HOT AND COLD

A COLLEGE HOCKEY ROMANCE

LESSON IN LOVE
BOOK THREE

TARA SEPTEMBER

Copyright © 2024

Editing by Joyce Mochrie with One Last Look.

1

———

JAX

FROM THE STARES and snickers trailing in my wake, you'd think I was the first teapot to ever walk across Thatcher College's beautiful New England campus.

All right. Yes, I just heard what I said. Muttering to myself like the lunatic I must appear to be, I pick up the pace and force myself to hold my head up. But all this seems to do is cause the bulbous costume I'm wearing to wiggle about my waist farther and lift the protruding spout higher into the air. So yeah, I probably look even more like a kettle that's about to boil over.

Here is my handle, here is my spout. When I get all steamed up, hear me shout—

As if reading my thoughts, some dude passing by calls out the last part of the nursery song, "Tip me over and pour me out," and his group of friends fall about themselves.

Ha ha, you're so clever. But I'll be the one with an extra $375 in my pocket at the end of the day, and I don't see them making that bread, thank you very much. Granted, the added humiliation was a bonus I wasn't counting on when I'd agreed to this campaign. My own stupid fault, though, as I was supposed to change into this tea-monstrosity once I was safely over at Diego's building, and only after I'd helped him with his film studies essay. Then, he said he'd record my paid TikTok idea for a new online tea subscription service that is sponsoring my account.

Which was all well and good, but then I had to go and try on this monstrosity ahead of time and ruin my sound plan. I just figured if I practiced the choreography while wearing the costume, it would cut the number of takes required later. Except … when it came time to remove the awful thing, it wouldn't budge, no matter how I wiggled, jumped, and rolled around on the floor of my dorm room. I think the clasp must be stuck to the black bodysuit I'm wearing underneath it. And of course, my roommate isn't here to help a girl out, and my normally bookish friends all seem to be MIA.

I'd sneaked down the empty Tasker dormitory stairwell and shuffled outside to my car with minimal attention. Before I could pat myself on the back, though, I belatedly realized that driving over to the sports house where Diego lives was no longer an option. I only wish I had figured that out before I struggled to stuff myself into the front seat of my Kia, only to have the costume ride up around my face, blocking all visibility.

After resembling an experimental performing artist exiting a clown car, I accepted the forgone conclusion I was going to have to walk the mile of shame to Diego's instead. It was either that or rip apart the teapot, which I have every intention of doing, but only after I get my skit recorded. Then, all this humiliation and frustration will be worth it. Almost.

So, despite the early November chill, I'm sweating

bullets in this getup as I waddle across the courtyard and wave jauntily at yet another cell phone being lifted to record my misery before wobbling up the steps of the two-story colonial home on the edge of campus. I've never been inside the building, even though I've been sort of seeing Diego, a soccer player and fellow junior in my film studies class. Then again, it's more like we've been hanging out, nothing serious. We've gone to a few parties together, which Diego considers "dates," and he tagged along with my friends to see the Leonid meteor shower last week, but honestly, I think we're nearing our expiration date.

Thank you, next! That's been my relationship motto, and I don't care what anyone thinks. I've never been one to make a quick purchase, so naturally, I've been trying out different guys like I do the outfits in my popular fashion try-on videos, which got me this influencer gig to begin with. My fashion fails do especially well, and I'm hoping this absurd teapot bit will bring me to the attention of other brands that may want to collaborate. Cha-ching!

Diego has been supportive and patient with my video requests, even gladly appearing in one. Although, I think he enjoyed the attention he received in the comments from my followers more than wanting to help me out. Kind of like our so-called relationship, we seem to be mainly for show. Time to shit or get off the pot, as my granny would so eloquently say. Or teapot, in my current state. I snort, proud of myself for still being able to make a joke right now.

Heaving a breath of relief, I rasp my knuckles on the wooden door, hoping Diego will answer and not one of the two dozen other athletes who live inside the catch-all sports house. After a moment of standing there like a fool, I knock again, more forcefully. That's right, I've never claimed to possess the virtue of patience.

What feels like an eternity later, the door swings open and I'm ready to stuff myself through the doorway and out of sight, but all I can see is the wall of a man's chest blocking my way. Glancing slowly up, a long way up, I meet the coolest blue eyes I've ever seen.

Automatically, I take a step back. Although we've never met, I know the icy stare belongs to none other than senior Luke Prescott, a.k.a. "Ice Man." A nickname given to him not only because he's the captain of Thatcher's legendary ice hockey team, but because of his chilly personality, hard-as-ice body, and equally thick … ego.

Well, Ice Man, step aside because this teapot is ready to spill the tea.

2

———

LUKE

As far as teapots go, she's easily the cutest one I've ever seen. My lips twitch as I take in the flustered brunette in front of me. Of all the things I was expecting when answering the loud bangs being belted upon our front door, this sure as hell was not one of them.

"Are you some sort of singing telegram?" I've never seen one before, except in old sitcoms that my parents used to watch, but it's the first thing that comes to mind. Because why else?

"Nope, can't sing," she says in a sassy voice. This one is no pushover, and for some unknown reason, I approve. Still, she doesn't seem to want to elaborate further on why she's knocking on doors dressed like Mrs. Potts.

"The theater department is on the other side of campus," I inform her, but the dozens of dirty cleats and smelly sneakers discarded on our porch should have tipped her off that this isn't the drama building.

She shakes her head, and I notice her hair is more reddish brown and her smile is kind of crooked, but again, she supplies nothing more. "A door-to-door tea missionary?" I ponder out loud. "If so, you will not convert me. I'm a black coffee kind of guy."

She snort-laughs without an ounce of pretense, and again, I am taken aback by this unexpected visitor with a killer smile, which she just turned the voltage up on. I almost … almost have to catch my breath at the sight of it.

"I'm sorry I'm not your 'cup of tea,'" she says using air quotes, her costume swooshing across the door's frame in the process.

I'll admit, her response is clever, and I allow myself a silent chuckle. "Well, Halloween was last month, and I'm plain out of guesses. What do you want?" I demand, and she stiffens, standing straighter.

The question came out harsher than I intended, but sorry. I'm not used to having a conversation with a teapot in the middle of the afternoon—or ever. I also have about a million things to do, and I'd already have gone back inside if this random teapot hadn't aroused my curiosity … among other things.

"Diego is expecting me," she says primly, and I have no idea why I know this, but I suspect there is nothing prim about the hellfire before me. I also doubt mister I'm-too-cool-for-school Diego is expecting this. Nor do I think it's a sexual role-play he'd be into, or frankly, any guy, really. The resulting images coming to my mind are just plain ridiculous, and I'm not sure how I'm able to keep a straight face.

"Diego?" I mutter, scratching my head, stalling as I try my best to puzzle together the mystery of the Thatcher teapot, which sounds like the title of a children's chapter book.

"Yes," she nods vigorously, which causes the foamlike handle on her costume to smack me this time. "Now, if you'll move out of the way so I can—"

"Go hide in a cupboard?" I suggest with a grin, and she snorts again.

"Maybe not a cupboard, but I wouldn't mind escaping inside," she says, shooting me an imploring, move-out-of-my-way-already look. When she moves forward, I step left and block her entry, her spout colliding with my body.

I stifle a laugh because if she thinks the hazel stink eye she's giving me is intimidation, she wouldn't make it past the puck drop. "Sorry, no girls allowed."

"Excuse me?" she questions, scrunching up her pert nose.

"No girls or teapots allowed," I repeat, and she bursts out laughing as if I just made a joke.

After another moment passes into our standoff, she straightens, obviously realizing I'm dead serious. She places an impatient hand on her other hip, and now it looks like she has two handles, one fake and one real. "It's not like I'm here to pledge," she says haughtily.

I roll my eyes. "This is an academic house for athletes, not a fraternity."

"I know," she sputters, "but you knew what I meant. Whatever. I'm here to help Diego study."

Now I've heard it all. Folding my arms across my chest, I give teapot an actual demonstration of intimidation. "Sure, you are, because D-Nasty is the studious type." My remark elicits one dark, feminine eyebrow arching in reply. "Oh, you didn't know your boyfriend's nickname? Yup, he's a real catch, that one," I say, pointing a thumb behind me, not bothering to hide my annoyance.

Being the gatekeeper isn't always fun, but as president of this house, it's my responsibility to keep the guys focused on their studies and training. As a result, I've had to set some strict rules, and that includes keeping the puck bunnies and jersey chasers out. Because while the residents can party and mess their lives up all they want, they just can't do it here.

"He's not my boyfriend," she retorts, and for some reason, the tightness in my chest eases. Her confident expression meanwhile crumbles in confusion. I can only describe it as witnessing some sort of internal battle. Every emotion possible plays across her pretty face. "We're just …"

If she says study partners, I'm going to slam the door shut, no matter how expressive her face is. I have stuff to do, and I'm not buying that load of bull for another minute. I don't know why I haven't walked away yet, except for some reason, I need to know what this girl is going to come out with next.

"We're not, just a date here and there," she says, babbling on. "He's pretty much my photographer whom I sometimes make out with," she explains wide-eyed, before quickly covering her mouth with her hands. "My God, why did I just tell you all of that?"

I've been wondering the same thing.

She chuckles, looking up at me with eyes that seem to sparkle. "I guess someone poured truth serum into this pot of tea."

Her self-deprecating laugh is almost contagious, but rules are rules, and Diego is two points away from getting kicked off the soccer team due to his shitty grades, which, in turn, jeopardizes our house's overall academic average. And I'll be damned if we lose campus funding while on my watch.

"Whatever. I don't care. He can't come out to play right now. He's finally working on an essay that's due tomorrow." I start to close the door as I should have done ten minutes ago.

"I'm serious," she shouts back. Faster than I expected,

she places a Converse-clad foot in the doorway, preventing it from shutting. Once again, I bite back a smile at her spunk.

"Yeah, you look serious," I quip, but she ignores the insult toward her attire.

"That's why I'm here … to help him with his essay."

Despite my better judgment and supposed lack of interest, I wave a hand toward her costume. "And you always attend 'study sessions' dressed like that?"

She releases a long-suffering sigh, and this time, I do smile, even if it feels rusty. I guess I'm enjoying myself more than I realized.

"Of course not. I need to film a dance skit in this thing, but the zipper is stuck and I can't get it off." I know who I'd like to get off, and I'm staring right at her while she continues to talk a mile a minute with temper flares sparking in her bewitching eyes. "So, instead of glaring at me like a prison guard on a power trip, can you please let me in already or go get Diego?"

"D-Nasty!" I shout, briefly turning my back on her to direct my yell upstairs to where I last left him working with the others. "It's teatime!"

"Huh?" comes a muffled reply in the distance.

"You have a visitor!" I call out again, then rotate back to the whiskey in a teacup who has since mimicked my crossed-arm stance. Nice try, but her puny scowl and silly costume ruin the whole effect. "Turn around," I command, twirling my finger in a circle. I can tell she's about to bite my head off again, so I explain myself, which is something else I'm not used to doing. "Let me see the back. Maybe I can help." With that said, the steam goes right out of her. And I swear, I didn't mean to make a tea reference that time.

She turns, sweeping her thick, wavy, brown hair with

hints of chestnut up and out of the way so I can examine the snagged zipper. I didn't even realize I knew the color chestnut, but it's what popped to mind when she lifted her hand to shove her rich locks away. With difficulty, I drag my gaze from her terrific tangle of hair.

There's a tear at the seam of her costume, and although I can see where it's hooked on the fabric underneath, my eyes seem to focus on her creamy, smooth nape instead. She has a cute freckle behind her ear too. Maybe it's been a hot minute, but my nostrils hone in on the fact that she even smells like jasmine tea. My fingers fumble for a second before unclipping the snarled snag, but once free, the costume immediately slips down to her knees.

"Oh, thank goodness!" she exclaims with relief, stepping out of it and leaving the shell of the teapot to lie there on the porch floor.

I can't say *I'm* relieved though. Because holy shit! She's dressed in a one-piece, black leotard that leaves nothing to the imagination, stretching tightly over her body like a second skin. Revealing a lusciously curvy body that would be any guy's dream to touch.

"Hey, babe," Diego cuts in, providing me with an opportunity to roll in my tongue. Stepping forward, he kisses her quickly on the lips and smacks her butt, causing her to yelp in shock. Study friends, my ass! "Glad you're here. Come on in, beautiful," he says, all charm.

With years of playing both offense and defense under my belt, my arm jolts out across the doorframe, blocking either of them from proceeding inside. "You know the rules—no girls during study time or for sleepovers."

Diego scoffs, not the least bit alarmed, but he sure as fuck should be. I'm at least six inches taller with way more muscle too. I shake my head. His inability to size up the competition is just one of the many reasons why Diego won't be making it on an MLS team after college and why he should be inside studying instead. It's what my parents taught me and what I'm always telling him and the other guys upstairs. You need to have a fallback. But D-Nasty thinks he knows it all.

"Dude, I told you earlier my buddy Jack was coming to help me with my stupid essay," Diego grumbles.

"*This* is Jack?'"

All right, so I didn't see that coming, and I shoot my gaze back at Diego's so-called buddy. The former teapot, "Jack," is grinning sweetly at our exchange, clearly relishing my shock. For some odd reason, I have the sudden urge to kiss her lopsided smirk away, which doesn't make any sense. I don't do impulsive, on or off the ice. Not anymore.

"It's Jacquie, Jacquelyn, Jack, or Jax with an x. Doesn't matter to me," she says, holding out a dainty hand in introduction.

"Fine, you got one hour," I allow, backing away from the doorway, leaving her hanging as I turn to Diego. "Next time, you better make it clear that your buddy is a chick."

I'm extremely doubtful any lady friend Diego would be interested in could possibly help with his abysmal grades, but he sure can use the apple, a.k.a. an assist. And at this point, we're down to a Hail "Jack" it seems.

3

JAX

SURE, some may consider it flighty or downright indecisive that I've tried out five different majors so far at Thatcher, but my mom and I prefer to call it being choosy. During my twenty-one years of life, we've tried out almost every state to live in except twenty, but I hope to explore those one day too. Now, after three years of college, I've finally declared an official subject—communications with a concentration in social media. It's what I'm good at and am passionate about, so I'm not sure why it took me so long to figure it out. I guess I just wanted to be sure. Really sure.

Besides, it's not as if my previous courses in psychology, political science, social work, and paleontology will go to waste. Okay, maybe the last one is a stretch since, unfortunately, there doesn't seem to be a real *Jurassic Park* opening anytime soon. But that's the point of attending a liberal arts college like Thatcher—to develop an appreciation for many subjects so you can pursue all sorts of careers after graduating. Right? Right!

I owe my final decision to the inspiring woman lecturing in front of our classroom, Professor Clark. Her Communications 101 and digital media courses last year opened my eyes to the fact that I could make a living doing what I already do every day, and not just as a hobby. The best part is that the small workshop I'm in now is exclusively for business and communications majors, and it also includes an epic, hands-on campus project. Each year, the student with the best results is awarded a summer internship with one of Clark's many illustrious alumni connections. Previously, winners have had the opportunity to intern for Amazon, the New England Patriots, and Dunkin brands, just to name a few.

The internship isn't only a resume builder but comes with summer housing, too, which means if I won, I wouldn't have to travel to San Diego to crash with my mom and her new naval boyfriend. Granted, he's supposedly some big-deal officer, not a young recruit, but I'd rather not spend my break playing twenty questions getting to know her latest entanglement. All the more reason why I need this opportunity. No matter what, this year, the winning student will be me. I'm going to make sure of it. I haven't felt such a fire under me since … well, I'm not sure when, but it's exciting! I sit taller in my seat, my stomach jittery with anticipation. This is what it must feel like going after your dreams. Bring it!

"I firmly believe in the power of real-world experience," Clark states loudly from behind her podium as though she's holding a press conference. She commands attention with ease, her many years of public speaking keeping us hanging on her every word, especially today though. Today, we receive our special campus assignments, and I'm so eager that I'm nodding along to her speech like a broken bobblehead toy. "As discussed," Clark continues, "you will each be working on an area of concern here at our fine school."

Oh, please … please don't let my task be something boring like publicizing this year's science fair. I don't know how my friend Emerson dragged me to her last competition, but after I realized we were long past the days of erupting baking soda volcanos, it was too late to escape. Instead, I had to hear about the perils of testing the DNA in a stool sample. I ended up skipping dinner that night. Yeah, I know STEM, or is it STEAM, is all the rage career wise, and Emerson will likely make more money than I ever will, but no, ma'am, no thank you. I was born to be creative, or at least that's the mantra I keep repeating in my head as if I'm taking shots filled with self-confidence.

"When I call your name, please come forward to collect your assignment, which I've painstakingly handpicked for each and every one of you. Not only will your challenge play off your abilities, it will also strengthen your weaknesses," Clark says, holding a stack of manila envelopes in her hand. "Inside your folder, you will find a brief backgrounder on the problem that needs to be addressed, as well as your point of contact. In lieu of a class lecture each week, moving forward, we will be meeting as a group to brainstorm ideas and to discuss your findings because, while your issues might be different, we can all learn from one another. However, it will be up to you alone to create a full communications plan, execute it professionally, and provide results."

My head continues to bob in eager agreement. Finally, Professor Clark ends the buildup and begins her roll call in alphabetical order by last name. It's not until hotshot senior Cal Chase from the track team turns around in his seat with an arched eyebrow that I realize I'm anxiously tapping my pencil on my desk.

I stop the action immediately. "My bad," I whisper, and he grins. I'd be smiling, too, if both my names started with a C. As expected, he's next to be called, and he bounds up to the front of the room, reaching out for his assignment as if it's a baton in one of his relay races.

Several more students are called up, and I'm about to snap my pencil in frustration. "Jacquie Silva!" Clark at last calls out, and somehow, I force myself not to race forward like the roadrunner cartoon.

It might be wishful thinking on my part, but I swear Clark gives me a secret smile as she extends the last remaining folder out to me. "I think you'll have fun with this one," she adds, and I thank her as I take the outstretched envelope and head back to my seat.

The classroom is now full of murmurs and shuffling papers. With great effort on my part, I manage not to rip the folio open. Slipping out the printed sheets, I quickly skim its contents, and joyous relief courses through me.

I've been tasked with raising awareness for Thatcher's prestigious hockey team—the Thatcher Thunderblades—which regrettably has declined in popularity over the years compared to other sports on campus. My goal will be to drive student support and to elevate the team's reputation so Thatcher can continue to lure incoming talent away from competing universities.

A million ideas fly to mind, and my heart is racing as though I had a double shot of espresso. I might not know much about the sport, but I know I can promote the shit out of it. Yup, this is going to be a slam dunk! I mean, a goal? Whatever. It's on! First step will be to get the word out about the team's achievements, its players, and pack the stadium. Or is it an arena? Oh my gosh, this is going to be so much fun!

My little in-seat victory dance halts the moment I flip to the last page and see one point of contact listed—Thunderblades' team captain, Luke Prescott.

4

JAX

"My internship can't come down to the Ice Man!" I whine to my friends later at lunch. Despite our different class schedules, we're usually able to eat together most afternoons, and today, I'm especially thankful as I need to vent.

"Luke Prescott?" my gal pal April Harris asks, stealing a nacho chip off my plate. "Six foot something, two hundred pounds of muscle, with dirty-blond hair flowing out of his helmet like some sort of Greek God?"

I grunt in annoyance. His nickname might be ice, but Luke is unarguably hot. Still, I'm surprised because I've never heard April gush about any guy who wasn't a fictional one set in the books she reads. I go with it, though, adding, "I'd say his hair is more light brown than dirty blond, and you forgot to mention his crystal-blue eyes."

Ice-cool eyes that tended to look intense, even when he smiled. Not that Luke did much of that.

"Oh, I was getting to those," April says with a goofy smile, totally missing the fact that I was going for sarcasm there. "He's always reminded me of the brooding

Heathcliff." Her faraway look tells me she's back to her favorite subject. I just hope one of her lengthy lit lectures doesn't follow.

"April, honey," Emerson pipes in with a soft voice meant to soothe someone who may or may not be crazy. "You know, half the time we have no idea what you're talking about."

"*Wuthering Heights*! You guys haven't read it yet? It's on the syllabus for McClure's class."

Emerson straightens, never one to miss a deadline or disappoint a teacher. "Not for another month, and I'm still trudging through Thoreau."

I keep quiet, not wanting to admit that I've downloaded the audiobook version and have yet to hit play either. Give me a break. The class fulfills a history and English requirement. It's not a passion like it is for April. And if it wasn't for Professor McClure being eye candy, I would never have let my pushy friend talk me into taking the dual course.

"Well, you'll understand what I mean once you read it," April adds, and we both nod, eager to change the subject, but our friend moves on quicker than we do. "Anyway, considering how popular and good-looking Luke is, you have to admire the guy for not being remotely interested in doing anything social on campus. Obstinately so. Hmm ... now that I think about it, he sounds like Emerson and me."

"Hey!" Emerson says, pushing the brim of her glasses up with her middle finger. "Fair enough," she concedes with a slight smirk, and we all laugh. My girls are proud to be bookworms and homebodies, but lately, I can't seem to keep track of them anymore. Something seems to be in the air our junior year.

But returning to my problem—the hockey grump who

caused goose bumps to break out over my skin just from the mere brush of his calloused hands on the back of my neck. His help undressing me the other day felt way more intimate than it should have, given the fact that he was simply removing a giant costume and not my actual clothes. But wow, I'm lucky I didn't fall to my knees along with the teapot.

And so, what if I felt that invisible zap of male–female awareness when I saw him? Big deal! I've felt that intangible connection before, and more times than I can count, it amounted to just that—a stupid zing of misplaced mutual attraction that soon fizzled out. "It doesn't matter how tall or gorgeous he is," I tell them, although it feels like I might be trying to warn myself too. "He's a tyrant, and I doubt he'll go along with any of the attention-driving stunts I've come up with, and without those, my plan is just basic. Nothing to win an internship over."

April sniffs, and I turn to look at her. She's squinting her green eyes in thought, and I ready myself for a friendly battle. April has a way of getting information out of people. I've often thought she'd make a great lawyer or an investigative journalist if she wasn't head over heels in love with English Literature.

"I think you're just put out that he's not acting like one of your usual lovestruck puppies. What was the name of that one guy who literally followed you everywhere? Mike?" April ponders aloud but doesn't bother letting me answer, or I'd have informed her that his name is Micah, not Mike, and that was freshman year. Ancient history. "So many beautiful girls and guys have crashed and burned throwing themselves at Luke, but nada. He's too focused to care or be polite about his rejections either. And everyone says he received offers from the NHL but turned them down to graduate first." She says this last part with a bit of awe. "If he has that kind of willpower and dedication to his studies, yeah, you might have a hard time with this one, Jax."

"No shit!" I grumble, her observation being as useful as a screen door on a submarine. But I suppose April does make a good point. I do like being in control, and from what I've witnessed and heard, so does Luke. Talk about heads butting. I'd like to say that it's nothing I can't handle, but I've yet to hear of anyone beating the Ice Man in or off the rink.

"But since you're going to be promoting his team, it only behooves him to help," Emerson supplies, ever the mediator.

"Yeah, right. He wouldn't even let me inside his stupid house to *help* Diego." I stab a fork in my salad with more force than needed. I couldn't decide if I should eat healthy today or enjoy life and chow down on what I really wanted —tacos. In the end, I went with a taco salad. Best of both worlds, even if the calorie count is probably the same, but calling it a salad makes me feel better about it at least. Like they say in my new chosen career field, it's all how you spin it.

"I saw your tea dance video," April adds with a snigger. "I'm not sure I would have let you in my house either."

Emerson smothers a laugh without providing her take on my costume or video, which currently has over twenty thousand views, so hardy har har.

"Didn't he used to date Theta president Morgan Hyatt?" questions Emerson. I nod, picturing the sorority leader, who just happens to be the most beautiful girl on campus. Hell, *I* have a girl crush on her. Although, I swear, that girl thinks the sun comes up just to hear her crow. Another one of my granny's classic sayings.

"But," Emerson continues, "I remember hearing

something about them breaking up once he backed out of the draft and left whichever fraternity he was in."

Phi Pike. I nod, recalling that bit of campus gossip too. "That was a year before the three of us got here, so who really knows what's true. Maybe the NHL stuff was just rumor?" One thing is for sure though. Something happened his freshman year to turn Luke into the anti-social Ice Man. I just wonder if he can be thawed enough to find out. Not just for mere curiosity's sake either. No, I'll need to know Luke better if I'm going to be able to promote both him and his team successfully. As Professor Clark loves to say ad nauseam—know your brand!

"I've never seen him play, but we had chemistry together last year," Emerson informs us. "He's a pre-med student and pretty brilliant. I bet he'll see the value in your project, Jax."

I roll my eyes at Emerson's matter-of-fact outlook. Smart equals nice in her mind, even if someone is clearly an unfriendly jerk. "Did he even talk to you or anyone in that class?"

"No," Emerson admits, "but neither did I. It's a critical science course, not a social hour."

The two of them would make a perfect couple, but for some reason, the errant thought doesn't sit well with me. "And now you have 'chemistry' with Steely Nash," I point out with a teasing wiggle of my eyebrows, totally enjoying seeing my overly private friend squirm for a change.

"Very funny," Emerson says, adjusting her glasses but not meeting my eyes.

Our sweet and serious Emerson shocked the hell out of us last month revealing that she not only knew "Steel," the sinfully sexy son of the uber-famous rocker Diesel, but that they were also teaming up on her not-so-secret list of college experiences that she wants to fulfill. Who knew?

Apparently, she's not so introverted after all, thanks to Steel's influence. He's done what her two besties couldn't, I guess. Just last weekend, Em even attended a sorority luau with him. Her first-ever college party, never mind a sought-after one on Greek Row.

Granted, I'd gone to that party, too, but with Diego, who got wasted and disappeared. Some date! I'm so glad I officially ended things with him. I probably shouldn't have done it over text, but not that he was beat-up about it either. It went like this:

> Diego: Wanna mess around? 🥒

> Me: I think we should just be friends.

> Aight, that's cool. Later.

> Later, gator 🐊

> Lol. You're so weird. Hot, but weird.

No idea why I added the corny gator part, but if that's my biggest regret when it comes to Diego, then I'm glad we're done.

"What's Cal's assignment?" April asks, bringing me back to the conversation at hand.

"Your neighbor Cal Chase, the one you supposedly hate? Why?" I reply before breaking off the tortilla shell and stuffing it into my mouth.

"No reason, just curious," April says, trying to sound nonchalant, but she's not fooling anyone at the table. "And I never used the word 'hate.'"

"Ha! Then why did you rip me a new one when I'd innocently invited him on our meteor shower outing?" I point out in my defense, but I'm glad Cal has been brought up. "Now that you mention him, though, I was surprised he didn't get my assignment, considering he's the athlete in our class."

"Yeah … so what *did* he get?" April demands, her bob haircut bouncing as she shakes her head in frustration. And I thought I had no patience? In comparison, April's quick-to-rise temper makes me seem like a saint. Who knew so much gumption could be packed into such a small package? She might look petite and sweet, but so are gremlins before they turn, which is why Emerson and I do our best not to provoke the surly beast within April if we can help it. Although, I don't have Emerson's success rate.

I lean in closer to the table, stalling further just to be a pain in April's ass. "How many times have we almost been sideswiped by a car while crossing Main Street due to the poor street lighting and faded crosswalk?"

"Dozens of times," Emerson chimes in with interest. "Seriously, it's so dangerous."

I nod. "Thankfully, the administration has called for better safety measures. So, Cal's working on a plan with campus security to suggest what technology and protocols should be implemented and then how to get the word out about the new rules. Professor Clark figured it would be easier for him since he's on the track team."

"How so?" April asks, unable to hide her curiosity, which is what I was counting on.

"Because he runs all over our campus and has races at other liberal arts colleges so he can observe their setup. I already heard him enlisting the Environmental Club to discuss solar lighting options." I pause, slumping in my seat. "Honestly, I think he's my biggest competition for the internship program."

"You don't have to worry about him," April says confidently, clearly knowing something I don't. "Like Luke, Cal is a senior, and he's already had a big summer internship at a popular marketing firm in New York City. He'll probably want to continue there or pursue a real position after he graduates, not another internship."

I hadn't thought about that, but it makes sense. "You're right!"

"Always," April answers smugly, and I'm tempted to point out that she's not right about her notion that Cal is a player, but I bite my tongue. If she wants to keep her nose in a book and pretend that she isn't interested in the hunky runner, then by all means. Nevertheless, I've been doing my best to nudge her in the right direction, which is just on the other side of her dorm room wall. "Hold up. How do you know about Cal's previous internship?"

Not so haughty now, April darts her catlike eyes from Emerson to me. "Um … we've been talking a little bit."

Finally! Emerson and I exchange a knowing look, which of course our overly observant friend doesn't miss. "Don't go there, you two. We're neighbors, so it's not like I can ignore him completely," she grumbles, gathering her ever-present stack of books before rising to leave. It's not often that Emerson and I get to tease April back, and we both giggle as she fumes out of the upper campus dining hall without bothering to look back.

5

LUKE

FOR SOME REASON, I'm not even surprised when I open the front door and see the fiery bombshell standing impatiently on the other side again. Although, I'm kinda bummed she's not wearing a banana costume or something equally ridiculous this time.

No, today, Jacquie, or should I call her Jax? Whatever. She's dressed in a pair of ripped jeans and a plain, beige turtleneck that emphasizes her sizeable breasts, but I don't let my gaze linger there … for too long. It's hard not to stare at her though. Her body is a curvy handful, and damn, do I want to handle it. Fuck.

She's even more beautiful than I remember. In that adorable, plucky sort of way. And I'd be lying if I said I haven't been thinking about her since that first unexpected visit. I even had the weirdest dream slash nightmare involving tea service.

Stupid Diego. He knows the rules, and Jax shouldn't be here no matter how amusing and mouthwatering she may be. She's a distraction. Plain and simple. Or *un*-plain and complicated in Jax's case. I'm always telling my teammates, don't get serious with a girl at this pivotal time in their lives, but they aren't of the same mind on this point. No, they're too busy thinking with their other head. Been there, done that.

"You again?" I gruff out, enjoying my gatekeeper role for a second time. Her hair is pulled back into a tight and serious ponytail, and she is wearing an "I mean business" expression that is laughable.

"Yes, I'm here to see—" she starts to explain, but I cut her off before she can say his name.

"I told you last time, no girls allowed. You can meet up with Diego someplace else."

"I'm not here to see Diego." If I were the jealous type, I might be a bit perturbed at how often Diego's name crosses her lush lips.

"Oh yeah?" I ask, sounding bored, or was that disappointment in my voice? Maybe Jax is a jersey chaser after all. Not that I'm judging, but if so, heaven help the poor bastard inside who will have to deal with this feisty vixen next. "Who's the lucky guy?"

"You," she says with a jaunty finger gun aimed right at my chest.

Not much surprises me, but I swear, this girl has the uncanny ability to keep me guessing and eager to hear what she'll come out with next. "Me?"

"That's right," she says, placing a hand on her hip. I wonder if she knows how sexy being sassy is because she's got it going on there.

"I'm flattered," I say drolly, "but hit the road, *Jack*. I'm not interested."

What, not even a laugh? Oh well. I shrug my shoulders and she stomps her foot, causing the porch floorboards to creek in response. Not because this pissed off, barely 5'7" gal is particularly strong or anything, but I keep meaning to file a work order with Roland in maintenance to come inspect our rickety porch. Too many bruisers like me tramping in and out of here, and it's gotten to the point where I don't trust its integrity anymore.

"First of all, yes, you should be flattered," she says with a haughty sniff, "if what you were thinking were true. But I'm not here for you in that sort of way. We have work to do."

Again, I'm stumped, and I don't like the feeling. "Work?"

She takes a deep breath. "If you could stop being a great big ogre for one moment and let me in, I'll explain."

"Right this way, Princess Fiona," I quip, stepping aside while gallantly waving my hand for her to enter. It's the second time I break my "no girls allowed" rule, and both times for her. Hmm.

Jax steps across the doorway with a triumphant expression on her pretty face. As she brushes past me, her ponytail swings with each bouncy step she takes. It's wrong, but I want to tug on it. Serve the brat right for calling me an ogre. Although, it does seem fitting, especially with her cast as a beautiful princess. Dude! What's up with you lately? Shaking my head, I stuff my hands into the pockets of my mesh gym shorts instead. To my earlier point, I've only met her twice, and she's already a distraction that I don't need. This ogre is not looking for an unavailable princess, and between my pre-med courses and intense schedule of practices and matches, I have no time even if I were. Or if she wasn't seeing D-Nasty, that is.

Jax selects a seat in our first-floor common room like she's Goldilocks in a bear's den. The first armchair she considers has someone's unfolded laundry piled on it, so she sidesteps it. Her second choice for a seat has a pizza carton resting on it, which is gross because I can't remember the last time anyone ordered a pie. Finally, she gingerly sits down on the worn-out couch, keeping her back ramrod straight to avoid the dirty crew sock discarded on the headrest.

Brushing aside the Xbox controllers so they don't go up my ass, I sit down on the ancient but sturdy wooden coffee table in front of her. "Spill it," I demand, and even I can hear how brusque I sound. I guess I'm used to a houseful of monosyllabic guys and forget sometimes to tone it down, but then again, maybe if I turn it up, she'll leave me alone and I can get back to studying.

For some unknown reason, she seems to find me, or what I said, funny and laughs under her breath. Instead of getting on with it, though, Jax looks around the room for a moment, taking it all in before glancing down at the red folder she's been holding. Extending it out to me, I take it but wait for her to continue, not looking at whatever it is she just gave me.

My stare down works, and I don't have to wait much longer before she dives into a convoluted explanation that could have been summed up in one sentence. Outside of a professor's lecture, I don't think I've heard anyone, male or female, utter this many words at once. But in the end, her story boils down to one thing to me—the fact that I don't have time to deal with her "project," even if, for some reason, I've been named her point of contact.

"Well, good luck with that," I say, handing back the unopened folder.

"No, good luck to us," she insists. Yeah, I like spunk, but not when it's being used against me. I glare at her, yet Jax continues unfazed. "I spoke with Coach Tavish before coming over here. He's thrilled the communications department approved his request, and he said the team captain, that's you—" she says, pointing another finger gun at me.

"Obviously," I say, rolling my eyes.

"—would be more than happy to help in any way he can."

"*He* can't," I say firmly. And gee, thanks for the heads-up, Coach. He should be the one handling this shit. He's the one going on and on about our team being underrepresented on campus. And it's not like he's the one playing in the upcoming Eastern Conference or the one worrying about taking the MCAT exam in January.

Ignoring my protest, Jax crosses her arms, causing her breasts to plump up. "Tavish said he'll reserve the rink tomorrow after your team practice so that I can grab some footage of his star player," she says with a satisfied smirk.

I'm all for the extra ice time, but not if she plans to put me in a teapot costume or have me do some crazy social media stunt. Standing, I lift her easily from the couch with barely a tug on her arms. She comes up flying, her stunned face bumping into my chest.

For some reason, a chill runs up *my* arm from the tip of my fingers, where I'm holding her, all the way to my shoulder. That sort of tingly feeling you get when you hit your funny bone, but without the pain. I'd probably been sitting too long at my desk today. I should go for a run and stretch my stiff body. That will fix whatever that odd sensation was. Great, now I have to add jogging to my never-ending list of to-dos today.

Annoyed and overwhelmed, I release her abruptly but then reach back for her arm again since she's still unsteady on her feet. This time, I feel goose bumps rising and lifting the fine hairs on my arms from our touch. That's what I get for wearing a T-shirt and shorts in November. This old house is drafty, especially this time of year. And speaking of houses, Jax needs to leave this one—pronto—before any more odd sensations decide to make an appearance. More gently, I place my hand on her lower back and usher her to the door.

"I'll see you tomorrow," she says, throwing me an uncertain look from over her shoulder.

"No, you won't," I reply, mimicking her singsong voice. This causes her hazel eyes to narrow to slits.

"We'll see about that," she says, just before I shut the door on her stunned face.

6

LUKE

I saw and she won.

Jax has Coach Tavish and most likely every man with a heartbeat eating out of her hand. I'll be damned if it'll be me, too, but Coach is giving me no choice in the matter.

"I don't know much about this Insta TikTok ding-dong stuff, but if it puts butts in seats, then I'm all for it," Coach barked during our grueling practice earlier. "This is our best season in years, and we're in the Frost Fest Tournament thanks to you, but hardly anyone on campus even knows about it. With this being your last season, I need to be in a better position to recruit. A packed arena will go a long way in securing the budget needed to rebuild next year. Do it for the team."

"For the team," I repeat, gliding out onto the ice. I'm pissed that I'm not showered and back home studying already. No one seems to realize the amount of work it takes to be a student athlete, never mind one in the pre-med program. But the second my blades bite into the smoothed surface, a sereness like no other rolls over me. It's hypnotic. Thoughts of unfinished homework and deadlines fade away. All I hear now is the sound of my skates marking up the fresh sheet of ice.

Ksssh-ksssh-ksssh.

Checking the clock up on the scoreboard, I see I still have a few minutes before Jax is expected to arrive, so I use this opportunity to practice my floorball skills and puck flip tricks. The sort of horseplay stuff you don't always get to do during a real game, but when you can, the payoff is even sweeter.

"Wow, that's perfect! Can you do it again?" Jax is holding up her phone to record me, and I miss my shot. Instead, I hear the dreaded sound of puck bouncing off metal. Dammit.

"No worries, I need to get closer anyway," she calls out from the players' bench all cheery-like.

While not exactly in a costume this time, she's dressed over the top in head-to-toe Thatcher spirit, including a beanie with a pom-pom in our school colors—gold and scarlet. Her auburn hair beneath the wool cap hangs down in two long braids, giving her a sort of Scandinavian Swiss Miss look. It's both hot and adorable and likely not an accident. This girl knows what looks good on her. She is the epitome of curves and confidence. Her direct stare alone could wilt a weaker man, but that sure as hell isn't me.

"Stop right there!" I tell her, and she immediately freezes halfway to the opening in the sideboard. It's almost comical how serious she took my command. "No shoes on the ice," I clarify, and she huffs, easing her rigid stance.

"No shoes, no girls … is 'no' your favorite word?"

"No," I repeat sternly, and she laughs, then meets my gaze with a heart-melting smile. I don't mean *my* heart, of course, but I imagine it would again affect another man's if aimed at them. With a rare smile of my own, I point at the window by the food stand. "You can grab a pair of skates over at the counter. Just show your Thatcher ID, and they'll hook you up."

Jax nods and hurries off. This time, the puck sails right through the goal lines, and so do my next several shots.

"Now may I enter?" Jax calls out a few minutes later, amusement evident in her voice as she glances nervously down at her feet.

I know people find it awkward to wear skates, but at this point, I'm so used to them that I feel weird in regular shoes.

"Must be incredible to wield such power," Jax muses aloud, not bothering to wait for me to answer her previous request. "Seems I need your permission to enter campus houses, and now rinks too." Laughing, she clutches the sideboard railing in a death grip.

Gingerly, she places her white figure skates on the slippery ice, but her step is too big, and she immediately slides. Ramming her back up against the barrier, she miraculously manages to hold herself up somehow. The scene resembles Bambi's first time on a frozen lake, and I feel bad for insisting on the skates-only rule, but honestly, the alternative can be just as dangerous. I should have told her to grab a helmet too. Mine's discarded on the bench behind her, but the heavy thing would probably have her toppling over farther.

"They have skate trainers somewhere," I say, glancing around the rink, hoping to spot the plastic walkers that they have for new skaters.

Instead of waiting to find one, Jax suddenly pushes away from the wall and I soar forward, ready to catch her if needed. Her arms flail as she wildly grasps at air. And just when I realize I won't be able to make it to her in time, she kicks off using her toe pick and executes an expert spin, gracefully raising her arms up over her head. It's a perfect pirouette paired with a smug smirk.

Yup, she's gone and surprised me once again. Her lips curl into the sweetest smile and I have the urge to smile back, but my mouth is still open from shock.

"I was a junior figure skater," she boasts, her face beaming with unconcealed amusement. Clearly relishing the moment, she bows and skates over to meet me center rink. "Never make assumptions, Captain," she adds, childishly sticking out her tongue and skating backward.

"Believe me, from our few encounters, I can't assume anything and have no idea what to make of you, Jax."

She smiles again as if I've given her a compliment, and perhaps I did, in an odd way. But since it appears we're going to be teamed up for the rest of the season, I tell myself to behave and keep the lighthearted mood going—for the team, that is.

"Clean slate?" I ask, holding out my ungloved hand to her. My big grip easily engulfs her slim hand when she places it into my palm. Like last time, an unexpected jolt runs up my arm, and by the way Jax slips a little on the ice, I wonder if she felt the electric current too. I thought sparks like that only happened when standing on carpet, not ice. Our gazes meet and hold for a prolonged moment and … I got nothing. All thoughts seem to erase from my mind.

What the hell, Luke? Get a grip!

Right. Belatedly, I realize I'm still *gripping* her hand and let go.

She stares down at her empty hand, her mouth forming a surprised O shape. A couple of seconds tick by before she skates leisurely over to where I was fooling around when she first arrived. Not surprisingly, Jax speaks first. "I used to close my eyes and pretend I was flying," she recalls wistfully, stretching out her arms and skating in a circle around me to demonstrate. "But I haven't been on the ice in years," she amends, now sounding forlorn, yet she slowly smiles up at me and my breath hitches.

I clear my throat, hoping it will do the same for my jumbled thoughts too. "Why'd you give it up?" I ask, since it's obvious she loves being out on the ice almost as much as I do.

"I lived right across the street from a rink as a little girl. That's how I got started. But when my mom remarried, we moved out of state, and there wasn't a skating program around," Jax explains matter-of-factly.

I try to imagine the scenario reversed, with me having to give up hockey when I was younger, and nope, don't like that picture. My love of hockey is what saved my family for a while there. The game helped keep me busy throughout my mom's first battle with cancer, and it seemed to cheer her up to hear of my achievements too. Even my dad, who could care less about the sport, was thankful to be able to drop me off with my coach for hours while he worked to pay for the piling medical bills.

"That sucks," I commiserate, but she shrugs it off.

"It was just a hobby," Jax hedges, shooting me a look over her shoulder, and I'm just now realizing we've been doing a lap around the rink together, like we're on some teenage date or something. Only thing missing is us holding hands while crappy, boy-band music plays over the speakers. "But it sure feels great to be out here again."

I nod, blading away to pick up my stick near my discarded gear. I feel steadier and more myself simply by having it back in my grasp. "All right, so what's the plan?" I ask, turning to her.

Jax's face takes on a serious expression, then an eager

one. I tell you, this girl should never play poker. The table would be able to read every thought that crosses her beautiful face. "Yes, so all the other teams at Thatcher have an active social media with students and alumni following along. Even the improv group has a decent follower count. We need to do the same. No, scratch that. We need to do better … national attention!"

"Good speech, but how do you do it?"

"We. How do *we* do it," she corrects, not allowing me the chance to counter. "We're going to have to pull off a hat trick." Her random use of the hockey term has my eyebrows arching. "That's right. It's going to take you, me, and the team." She nods triumphantly, adding, "I've been studying up on the hockey lingo."

Before I can school her on what performing a hat trick really means, she's already talking and skating once again. "First, we'll feature the team, but especially you in fun, get-to-know-you type videos."

"Doesn't seem like that will go viral."

"Just leave the digital storytelling to me," Jax says with confidence, ignoring my naysaying and progressively skating backward. "I know how to make videos stand out. Plus, it helps that you're easy on the eyes." She says the last statement while comically batting her eyes.

I stop gliding. "What difference does that make?"

She laughs as if I'm joking. "The difference will be more women in the stands for your home games. Next, we'll share footage of cool shots like the ones you were doing earlier. Trick shot videos are more popular than ever." She continues talking and skating without missing a beat. "We pair the clips with trending music, and voilà." Pursing her lips, she stops mid-thought and mid-skate. Spinning around, she looks me up and down, and I'm immediately wary. "If you could lose your shirt, then even better."

"I will if you will," I goad without thinking. But damn! That stupid, expressive face of hers … I swear for a second, she's considering my dare.

"How about we start by both losing our hoodies, Ice Man?" she suggests, pulling at the hem of hers and lifting it up over her head before I can agree or not. Despite the chilly arena, I'm breaking out in a sweat.

"Hell, I'm game," I tell her, tearing off my stank practice hoodie and tossing it on top of the net, leaving me in just a skintight, moisture-wicking shirt that the school provided for warm-ups.

I drag in a thankful breath of the cool, fresh air. I'd rather be cold than hot, especially after looking at Jax, who's practically popping out of her shelf bra tank top. Unfortunately, the chilly air does nothing to combat the sudden fire coursing through my veins. The burning only increases when her golden gaze trails up and down *my* chest as she blatantly checks me out. When she's done with her perusal of me, she dares to lick her lips. Accident or not, it's causing the air to rush out of my lungs. Holy fuck! I'm both thankful and frustrated that I'm still wearing my jockstrap from practice because while the protective cup is shielding my reaction to her modest striptease, the plastic is also cutting off my circulation. *Good*, I think, gritting my teeth. The pain should take care of the situation soon enough. If only it could erase this attraction between us, too, so I can concentrate on my other Jax problem—her communications plan.

"I skimmed the proposal you shared with Coach," I tell her, while she records me doing a neat puck flip, like I'm tossing flapjacks before I send it sailing into the net.

"You did?" she says with unconcealed excitement in her voice. "It's just a draft."

I grunt in reply. "The intermission games sound fun. I've seen minor league teams have people come out on the ice to play beachball hockey and do relay races like that to keep the crowd entertained between periods."

"Exactly," she says. "Keeps the action moving and fun for the guests."

I nod, slapping another puck into the net. Yup, I admit some of the ideas she came up with are clever, while others are just plain ridiculous. "An ice cube's chance in hell I'm going to be auctioned off or pose for a stupid calendar. Imagine suggesting half of that shit to the women's hockey team?" I ask, ripping a shot off the crossbar. It's not even a clink. It's like a tiiinnng.

Unfazed by my accusation, Jax smiles at me before bending down to pick up my alternate hockey stick. "Are you calling me sexist?"

She tests the stick out by gently pushing a puck in front of her. Like me, the stick is too big for her. And if she continues to lean like that, her lower back will be sore come morning and, unfortunately, not from any of the dirty scenarios I've imagined over the last five minutes with our bodies tangled together.

"Valid," she responds to her own question, continuing the one-sided conversation, "but my ideas are not 'shit,' and I'm going for shock value anyway. The kind of PR stunts that will have the entire campus talking about Thatcher's hockey team again. But—," she draws out. Spinning around to face me, she almost smacks me with the butt end of the stick.

"Easy now," I say, batting it away. Again, she smiles, but this time it's sensual, and I almost forget what we are arguing about. Oh right, me becoming a pin-up model. H-E-double- hockey-sticks NO!

"How about a little bet?" she asks, throwing me off guard for about the hundredth time. I swear, following her convoluted thoughts is like playing a game of Chutes and Ladders. One minute, you're steadily marching up a ladder, only to be swooping down a slide toward the bottom of the board the next. Little miss bossy pants doesn't give me a second to respond, either, but given how her face is now lit up like a Christmas tree, I'm again suspicious.

"Why don't we have a shoot-out for the ideas you have issue with," she suggests all sugar and spice like. "If I score, it stays. If I miss, it's out."

Throwing my head back, my uncontrollable laughter echoes around the empty arena. She can't be serious. Most grown men are hard-pressed to get a puck past me, and this silly girl thinks she has a chance? Yeah, she can skate, but that doesn't mean she can play hockey.

Undeterred, Jax is gliding to the center circle like she was just awarded a penalty shot. "Go ahead, over there," she says, pointing the blade of her borrowed stick to where she wants me to stand. I humor her, but I don't bother assuming an actual defensive position. No, I goad her by crossing my arms and slouching back on the heels of my skates. It's my, I-don't-have-a-care-in-the-world stance, and right now, I suppose I don't.

Jax nods like she just gave herself some sort of internal pep talk. "This is for the date-a-player sale," she says, drawing the stick back too high. I don't flinch as it flies toward me, nor do I bother following the path of the puck to know she's missed the net. I could tell the moment she hit it that it was a dud. This is where I'd normally instruct a beginner that they need to snap their wrist while they shoot and transfer their weight forward. Even then, I doubt her measly one hundred ten pounds or so would make much difference, especially with her terrible lack of follow-through. I'm also in no mood to put my captain jersey back on and play coach.

"I guess I'm off the auction block," I say, passing another puck toward her, eager to continue watching this train wreck.

Jax brushes the loss off as if it's no biggie, and my protective instincts have me on guard. Something isn't adding up here.

"If my summers living in Reno with Peter taught me anything," she informs, "you never bet more than you can lose."

I try to unpack what she just said but am stuck on the most important part of her outrageous comment. "Peter?"

"Stepdad number two," she says, holding up two fingers. "He was a casino pit boss. So yeah, I started with that idea as a warm-up because I wasn't sure how PC the whole auction thing was anyway, and I was prepared to scrap it if needed. Now, come at me this time." She waves me forward with a teasing come-and-get-it motion with her right hand. My legs have me springing forward before my brain can finish digesting all of what she just shared. But hell, if her baiting and sheer unpredictability isn't turning me on. Cup, don't fail me now.

Jax moves left, and I easily do too. Then she darts right, and I lazily meet her again. This time, she does a neat spin and slips around me. "This is for the penalty box kissing booth!"

She shoots and misses. Her positivity seems to crack this time, and she throws me an agitated glare. It takes all of my concentration to bite back the smile that is threatening to break free. No need to add salt to her injury by gloating. I'm not a total dick, after all. But I really should end this game soon and put her out of her misery before there is no communications plan left. But a sadistic part of me is delighting in doing the opposite.

Her smile slips for a moment, then comes right back, more dazzling than ever. "Fine." She shrugs, neatly shifting her Thatcher beanie into place, the pom-pom on top flopping along with the action.

"Oh yeah, because that's going to make the difference," I tell her, unable to hold the barb in.

Jax raises her chin defiantly, and I gotta admit, her scowl is even sexier than her brilliant smiles. Determined, her small hands clutch tightly on the stick—like she truly believes she could score against me—even as the tops of her mouthwatering breasts strain against the thin fabric of her tank, her nipples hard, little points that I want to lean down and take into my mouth.

"Goal!"

Wait, what? I twist around to see Jax triumphantly holding my hockey stick over her head like she's Gandalf the wizard. I search for the puck, and sure enough, it's in the net, mocking me. I told you, nothing but a distraction. Yes, I'm arguing with myself now. Further proof that women are trouble.

"That was for the rubber ducky drop!" she declares, circling me in a satisfied, ass-wiggly glide. Damn. "We'll rig a net from the ceiling full of plastic ducks and drop it right after the first Thatcher goal is scored. Everyone will get to go grab a rubber duck as a keepsake, but there will also be different colored ones that will signal an additional prize for whoever snags those. Oh, but I was also thinking that the top ten people with the most social shares will get the chance to grab first, since they are helping spread the word for us."

I look up toward the scaffolding and lights above, processing it all. As if reading my thoughts, Jax adds, "I already talked to the backstage theater hands, and they agreed to take care of the mechanics of it."

I nod. "But what do ducks have to do with anything? We're the Thatcher Thunderblades!"

Jax laughs happily alongside me. "That's right, and we're going to make it rain ducks! It will be the great duck drop … like a puck drop, get it? Besides, it will make for a fun photo opp. And it's a free takeaway for those who lose too."

"And what do those with the colored prize ducks win?" I ask skeptically since Jax is back to skating with the sashay in her glide, which has my wary meter now pointing toward off the charts.

"Thunderblades' swag, I guess, but one lucky grand prize winner will receive season tickets right up against the glass."

I know what I'd like up against the glass. Jax in her cleavage-heightening tank top—and only that.

"And," she says, shooting me an innocent look that instantly clears my dirty vision, "a rinkside kiss from you."

"Me? Why not the player of their choice?"

She nods as if we're saying the same thing, which we're clearly not. "Awe, sweetie, how cute you think the winner isn't going to choose you, but okay, let's go with that." To further her point, she playfully slaps me on the ass with her stick.

I wish I could do the same with *MY* stick because it obviously has a mind to choose her. But in its defense, it's been a long, dry season, and we're only two months into it. Clearing my throat, I try my best to put my brain back in charge of thinking before I develop a full-blown hard-on.

"What if a guy wins?" I ask, trying to poke holes into her cockamamie prize selection.

Pausing, she seems to consider my question for a second. "Whatever, think big picture. These are all just semantics. Besides, if my friend Asif wins, get ready to still pucker up, buttercup! Otherwise, I guess the winner can get a kiss from one of the dancers instead … or hell, me if the spirit team isn't willing."

I'm not sure why the latter image pisses me off more than the thought of kissing a dude. "And this is for the calendar!" Jax calls out, ripping another puck past my skates and into the net.

"Wait!" I interject, "I wasn't ready." All right, teasing aside now, it's on!

"Don't worry, I'll let you choose your month, but I was envisioning a cold January scene for the legendary Ice Man."

"No way am I posing shirtless for a calendar!"

"Now, don't be a sore loser. A bet is a bet," she consoles with a sweet smirk, and it has my teeth grinding. "How else will we raise money for the cost of all those rubber duckies? Plus, it's free publicity. Every time someone spots the calendar hanging somewhere on campus, they'll be reminded that we do, in fact, have an amazing hockey team here at Thatcher. We can also have your home games pre-filled in, along with tournaments and conference schedules circled. Seriously, all modesty aside, it just makes sense."

"I'm not being modest," I grumble. "Who even uses wall calendars anymore anyway?"

"You're right!" Jax exclaims, crashing into my side when she fails to stop in her haste, or maybe she's purposely using me as a sort of bumper wall. Laughing, she pushes off my chest and slides back a few inches, so she can properly look up at me. Her hazel eyes are gleaming with enthusiasm. "We should offer a digital version, too, which ohhh will come with free mobile wallpapers."

My groan is loud enough to rumble through the empty rink, but Jax only chuckles, dropping the spare stick near the rest of my gear before leaving me in her chaotic wake.

"Wait, that's it? No rematch? What about the other bullet points?"

"We can settle those another time. I have to get going. Need to check with the Software & Coding Club to see if a digital version of the calendar is possible. Lots to do," she rambles without looking back. Then she practically hops off the ice and back through the players' entrance, resembling the spastic bunny from *Alice in Wonderland*. The one that was always late for an important date. Leaning down to unlace her skates, she calls out from the bench, "I'll see you for Saturday's game!"

"We're away," I shout back, relieved, for once, to be traveling, even if it means an uncomfortable, early bus ride before a tough matchup against Wittmore University.

"I know. I'm riding with you guys."

"Guys, being the key word there!"

"Let me guess … no girls allowed on the bus either?" she mocks, laughter clear in her voice.

"That's right! But it's Coach's rule, not mine."

Although her face is pointed downward, focused on the task of removing her remaining skate, I somehow know she's rolling her eyes in response. "We'll see," she says pleasantly over her shoulder as she exits.

God, but I'm starting to hate those two little words … we'll see.

Unless it's *seeing* Jax naked, I'm not interested. If only I could erase that pesky thought, too, and get back to focusing on what matters—hockey and my schoolwork.

That's all I have room for, not the confusing whirlwind that is Jacquie Silva and her wacky stunts and unpredictable conversations. Since meeting her, though, I keep needing to remind myself that women are off limits, despite what my dick thinks, but even I'm getting annoyed with my instructions.

With a snarl, I take out my frustration on the puck in front of me. This time when I whack it, it whizzes into the net with a satisfying hiss, but there is no one to witness it.

7

―――――――

JAX

I HEAVE a sigh of relief when I spot the team's luxury motorbus double-parked in the distance. Afraid it still might leave without me, I quickly spring out of my car and kick the door shut, all while balancing three pink boxes of donuts. First impressions are everything, and just because I blew my first couple of meetings with Luke, that doesn't mean I intend to do the same with the rest of the players.

Luckily, I managed to get Donut Stress, the new bakery shop in town, to donate these treats for the team in exchange for photos and tagging their socials. I thought it was a pretty sweet deal, literally! Sure, it's not the healthiest of breakfast options for athletes, but I doubt a group of hungry dudes will care. Especially considering it's only seven in the morning, and who couldn't use a little sugar rush to start the day?

Evidently, not Luke. The irritated look on his stupidly handsome face has me halting in my tracks and my smile faltering. He's glaring at the pink boxes like I'm carrying a bomb or something, and that's when I notice he's handing out granola bars to each player as they board.

"Oops," I say, approaching cautiously. "Haven't you ever heard of the expression, the more the merrier?"

"No," he says, repeating his favorite word. "How does it go?"

With an eye roll, I brush past the surly ogre and climb the steps of the bus. The interior already smells like sweaty men, and they haven't even had their match yet.

"Ah, there she is." Coach Tavish beams a smile from the front seat directly behind the driver. At least someone is happy to see me. "I told the crew to behave and to give you whatever you need," he says, waving a big hand over his shoulder to the rowdy bunch behind him.

"Thank you, Coach." Nodding, I flip open the top box and offer Tavish a fresh donut, which he happily accepts, unlike his star player, who I can hear huff with annoyance behind me. Even though he's on the step below, his exalted breath hits just behind my ear and sends a quick shiver through my body. Well, he can huff and puff all he wants, but this little piggy is not running home. Not that I meant to call myself a pig.

Swiveling back to Luke, I try again. "Come on, you know you want it," I coo.

It's only when his eyebrows slant upward that I realize it came out like an invitation to more than just the donuts I'm holding. Although not my intention, I roll with it and add a saucy wink for good measure.

"I can't," he says through gritted teeth.

"Sure you can," I tease. "It's literally a piece of cake … or dough, I guess."

"No," he returns for the umpteenth time, his gravelly voice sending a rush of goose bumps over my flesh.

Fine. I shoot him a glare and turn toward the other players, who are caught up in conversations among themselves and haven't noticed my intrusion on their team bus. I falter, temporarily unsure how to proceed among the pack. Summoning my biggest smile, I announce, "Hi, guys, who wants a donut?"

A wave of male heads turn in unison. Afraid that I might get mauled by the mob of eager athletes, I shove the open box into the outstretched arms of a large guy seated to my right and another box to a hairy dude on my left. "Take one and pass 'em down," I instruct, now walking down the aisle with the remaining box held firmly in my grip. "I'm Jax, by the way, your … marketing coach."

Amid their chewing and grabbing, a chorus of greetings fly my way. Their big grins, flirty once-overs, and head bobs have me almost blushing. A very attractive sophomore, who I think is named Tanner Bouché, shoots me a smile and says, "Hey, 'lil coach!" Yup, it appears the rumors are true—the hockey team's rizz game or charisma is as strong as their fit bodies.

That is, everyone's except the Lukeness Monster lumbering behind me. I don't even have to look over my shoulder to know he's probably scowling. Nope, I can feel it. Several of the guys I pass graciously stand to offer me their seat, but before I can make my selection, Luke's voice silences the crew. "She's sitting in the back with me."

His directive has them settling back down, and I'm soon forgotten by the group.

Gee, thanks, big brother! I swallow my indignation and head to what must be his spot—the only two empty seats left in the very back of the bus. I guess not even his teammates want to sit with the Ice Man. As I continue forward down the aisle, I overhear one guy grumbling to his seatmate, "He just wants the rest of the donuts for himself."

But his friend shakes his head and stage-whispers, "I don't think it's the donuts he's after," and everyone around us chuckles. Now I might actually be blushing this time because I can feel the heat creeping up my face at their false assumption.

Without another word, I flop down on the cushy bucket seat and slide toward the window. Placing the treats on my lap, I select a chocolate glazed for myself, then pass the last box to the pair in front of me, where it quickly disappears out of sight. Recalling that the bakery wanted a photo of the team eating their desserts, I grab my phone with my other hand and jump up again. "Everyone, can you please thank the folks at Donut Stress Bakery for their donation?"

On cue, the team smiles and holds up what remains of their donuts and the empty pink boxes. "Thank you," they practically sing together.

"Perfect!" I tell them, tapping the record button off. Easy-peasy. As a reward, I take a bite of my donut.

"Are you done? Or should we call the other team and tell them we forfeit because we have a morning photo shoot?" Luke hisses, sending an icy glare down at me through narrowed blue eyes. Eyes that tend to look intense, even when he smiles. Not that he does much of that, at least not around me.

Authoritative jerk! "I'm sorry if I delayed you one minute," I retort, not sure how anyone, besides my non-morning friend April, can be this disgruntled so early in the day. He really should have had a donut too. Maybe that would have sweetened him some. Eyeing him, I continue to munch on my treat and wave his hostility off with a flip of my wrist, which accidentally causes crumbs to cascade on his empty seat, so I hasten to brush them off.

As if the bus driver felt Luke's impatience, too, the bus lurches forward, and I drop my donut on the floor. Luke falls backward, depositing himself abruptly on his cranky ass. I bite the inside of my cheek to keep from laughing out loud while Luke growls his irritation. Seriously, he just growled low in his throat, like some hockey beast. Replaying his fall in my head on loop like a silly, animated gif has my shoulders shaking with silent laughter, which only makes Luke grumble more. I like to poke the bear, I guess, because really, I'm enjoying his testiness.

Leaning down, Luke picks up my fallen donut from the floor. As he hands me the powdery treat, our fingers brush and there's a jolt of electricity. The little thrill dances straight up my arm. Our eyes meet, and mine are likely as wide as his. When Luke clears his throat, we both hastily look away. Keeping busy, I wrap the dirty donut in a napkin and stuff it in the seat back pocket.

"Sooo," I draw out, wiggling the irritation knife deeper into the surly monster. "Over an hour trapped next to me. Are you sure you're up for it, Captain?"

Given Luke's alarmed expression, he obviously hadn't thought his seat assignment through. He mumbles something under his breath that I can't quite make out … something about what one part of him was. Then more clearly, I hear the words "pain in the ass."

Regardless, I choose to ignore it because you catch more bees with honey and all that. And I have a list of questions I need answers to, although the heat emanating from Luke's big body and his manly smell filling my nostrils has me fumbling to recall any of them. I swear, I think I just got high from inhaling him because all of a sudden, I'm light-headed. And when his arm brushes mine as he settles into his seat, goose bumps rise along my arms. You'd think I never sat next to a boy before. Then again, he's no boy, but all man, and I've never met anyone as controlled and unreadable as Luke. He has the whole tortured hero thing on lockdown. I'm just not sure what haunts him, though, besides my current pestering, that is.

"I … uh, I read on a hockey blog that you signed with one of the biggest sports agencies when you were still in high school." All of which begs the question, why wasn't Luke in the pros already? It was lucky I'd found that announcement, too, because Luke's social pages are all set to private, making my online stalking that much harder. No mutual friends either.

"The interrogation starts now?" Luke groans, pinching the bridge of his nose as if warding off a headache. "We haven't even left campus yet."

"Why not? We've got over an hour to kill," I say, nodding, and Luke releases a deep sigh, crossing his arms over his chest, which has his biceps bulging farther. Dragging my gaze away from the touchable sight, I focus on the bold number 22 inked on his upper arm, right where it would appear on the sleeve of his jersey if he had it on. Mesmerized, I almost jump when he finally speaks.

"You expect me to spill my guts to you or something?"

"Or something," I say, merrily watching Luke grit his teeth as I continue my chatter. "Just pretend I'm your shrink. You know, psychology was the first major I was considering at Thatcher. I even took all the 101 courses, doubling up over the summer to complete them, but in the end, it didn't feel like the right fit. I also fainted in class after watching a video about Phineas Gage's accident— you know, when the railroad spike goes through his skull— but miraculously, he's still able to retain most of his mental functions." I shiver just remembering the horror of seeing the reenactment and how I'd over-empathized and slank from my chair to the floor in the middle of class. Not much embarrasses me, but coming to and seeing everyone's concerned faces above me sure did.

"That was you?" Luke asks, goggling.

Ugh! Yeah, I almost forgot how the fainting girl was the talk of campus my freshman year. Poor Emerson still carries around smelling salts in her backpack just in case I pass out under her watch. Luckily, I haven't given her a reason to use them since. "Yup, you're sitting next to Thatcher's infamous fainting goat."

Luke chuckles, but it doesn't sound mean, at least. More sympathetic, kindred. I guess the Ice Man has a good bedside manner after all. "You're not going to believe this, but my professor assigned a research report on Vasovagal syncope after your incident. It might be genetic, but basically, it happens when the body overreacts to certain triggers, such as the sight of blood or extreme emotional distress."

"Tell me about it," I grumble. "I only wanted to work with the brain on an emotional level, not the physical, which is why I never even considered going into medicine like you."

"Don't worry, I know how to handle you … I mean, if you have another episode."

"I won't!" I assure him, although as for him handling me, I wouldn't object to that.

Luke grins. "Are you sure? There very well might be blood spilled at today's game."

"If it's your blood, I'll be fine," I respond drolly.

He chuckles and I join in. Our banter seems so easy, it's hard not to enjoy it.

"So," Luke drawls, "you moved on to communications next?"

"No. I tried out a few other career options first," I hedge.

"How many?"

"Five."

"Five?" Luke echoes, sounding alarmed. Given how his eyes have widened to the size of hockey pucks, you'd think I confessed to killing five people instead of five studies.

"Yes, but I'm done now. Communications *is* the one."

He cocks his head. "Well, you *do* like to communicate," Luke jokes, not bothering to hide his sarcasm.

"Good one," I tell him, refusing to let his grumpiness infect me. Oddly enough, it seems to make me want to divulge more. "Anyway, I'm the one who's supposed to be asking the questions here and getting to know you, not the other way around."

"I'm a free agent now," Luke murmurs, reminding me of my original inquiry.

Right. Focus, Jax. "What happened to the infamous sports agency you signed with?"

He lifts and lowers one shoulder. "They dropped me."

I gasp, insulted on his behalf. "But—but after your first season at Thatcher, you were already a first-round draft pick. I had to look up what all that means exactly, but yeah, it's a big deal." Luke nods, and his silky, not-quite-shoulder-length hair moves along with the action. He doesn't say anything further, though, and now I want to sigh in frustration too. We were just getting somewhere. "It doesn't make sense," I prod, nudging his side lightly with my elbow. But he's all muscle there, too, and I wonder if he even feels my puny poke.

"It does when your agent keeps turning down offers for you," Luke says matter-of-factly.

"Why did he turn them down?"

"Because I told him to."

"I don't get it."

Luke closes his eyes, no doubt hoping that it will somehow blot out the sound of my voice. With another sigh, Luke abandons his arms-crossed defensive position and sort of slumps in his seat in what I hope is acquiescence. "I made it clear to him I wouldn't entertain any offers till after I graduated."

"Why?"

Another huff through his nostrils. "Because I promised my mother that I'd get my degree first."

"Why?"

"Because I promised her," Luke echoes, absently tracing his tattoo with the pads of his fingertips.

"But why?"

Luke's resulting groan is so loud, his teammate Blake Halsey, seated diagonally from us, turns to check on his captain. But after seeing Luke's surly face, he immediately snaps his head forward like nothing happened. "If my favorite word is 'no,' yours is surely 'why.'"

I chuckle because he's not wrong there, and I'm relieved to see his lip lift into a small smile. Then again, it might be wishful thinking on my part, and it may very well be a scowl in disguise. I wisely move on to my next line of questioning just in case. "So, the Eastern Conference is major. You helped Thatcher qualify your freshman year, too, where you guys made it to the finals."

He shrugs the accomplishment off. "A final isn't a win. I'd love to bring home the championship banner this year."

I nod, recalling the division and tournament banners hanging proudly from the ceiling over the rink. "I bet you will. The chatter online gives Thatcher high odds."

Luke grunts, and I'm stunned when he elaborates further without any prompting on my part this time. "It's my last shot regardless, and many of the NHL scouts who were originally looking to draft me will be there to see if I'm still up to snuff."

"Can you sign up with them after the Frost Fest instead of waiting for the draft in the spring?"

"Yes and no. Once you sign a contract with an NHL team, you are no longer eligible to play in the NCAA, which is why I've held off. Now—"

"Now you're almost done with college and can maybe sign a contract," I say, too excited to stop myself from interrupting him. Just one of my many bad habits I need to work on. It's just always last on my list.

Luke doesn't say anything, but he's not denying it either. I scrutinize his unreadable face and can't tell if he's scared, excited, or just plain bored. He certainly doesn't look like a guy who's about to get offered an NHL contract. Where is the jubilation, the relief, the gloating? I guess it's not real yet, not until the fat lady sings or whatever the hockey equivalent is. If I were in his skates, I'd be doing victory high fives up and down this bus. Then again, I'd also be sick with worry to come this close and not make it. "Holy shit, but that is a lot of pressure," I say the thought aloud.

Luke shoots me a staggered, sideways glance. "You have no idea."

"I guess my competition for the internship program is low stakes in comparison."

"I don't know about that," Luke says, shaking his head. "Just different skill sets."

A tender warmth burns in the pit of my stomach at his defense. "Still, I'm not representing an entire college or performing for scouts. Just a mere professor."

"You want it, don't you? That's why you're riding this bus on an early Saturday morning, no?"

I nod, but Luke's shaking his head again. "Say it," he demands, his voice turning forceful.

Confused, I'm not sure what he's asking at first, but the fire burning in his cool-blue eyes answers my unspoken question. "I want it!" I say with enough power to cause a few of the players to twist in their seats. I think I might have woken up one angry-looking guy, and of course, he's the biggest player on the bus too. Oops.

"Then go get it!" Luke urges, as if it's that simple, and perhaps it is. With a release of breath, he adds begrudgingly, "I'll help you."

No more resistance from him? I have an urge to hug this lion of a man with hidden depths. "Really?" Impulsively, I grip his hand instead. My palm tingles in response, and when I look up at him, Luke is staring at me, but I can't read his expression. He seems almost puzzled. "Thank you!"

"I'll help, but I'm not doing the calendar though," he grumbles.

I wave a hand dismissively, too happy to ruin the moment by debating the merits of the calendar today. "We'll see."

"Not that again," he groans.

"What?"

"Nothing," he says, closing his eyes, most likely wishing he could close me out too. But I'm not deterred.

"Is the conference always over Thanksgiving break?"

He nods, eyes still closed. "Freshman year, my parents rented a hotel room with a little kitchenette, and my mother managed to cook up a turkey feast for us in it." A wistful smile softens his face as he recalls the memory. "She made turkey sandwiches for the whole team too."

"Aww, that's special. What are you guys doing this year?"

The smile falls away from his face, his whole body growing rigid as if my words magically turned him into a marble statue. His eyes, now open, look haunted, and I suck in air at the pain I see reflected there. I fumble for a way to correct my goof but fail to register what I'd said wrong, but Luke speaks first.

"My dad and my … uh … aunt Kathy are looking at going," he eventually says while staring blankly ahead, all signs of joking seeming to have left his voice.

Given the sneering way he'd said her name, he must not care for his aunt much. Just another puzzle piece to fit when I still haven't even completed the border. "And your mom?"

Luke stills impossibly further, except for one hand that he balls into a tight fist. "Not possible."

Ah, so that's why he's upset. Hell, I understand that. "I haven't spent a Thanksgiving with my mom since I went off to college," I share. "This year, she's headed to Portugal with her latest boyfriend. They invited me, but fourteen hours round trip is pretty far to go for just a long weekend."

"What are you gonna do for the holiday then?" he asks, his tone more relaxed now that we're not talking about him.

"Well, last year, I went home with my friend Emerson, but her dad is an uptight principal, and their house was like living in a study hall." An internal shutter runs through me simply remembering how chilly and boring it had been there. "I'll probably sign up to remain on campus."

The bus hits a pothole bigger than Luke, and if he wasn't seated next to me like a sturdy bookend, I'd likely have been flung out into the aisle like a rag doll. Instead, he got rammed with some side boob. As covertly as possible, I try to adjust myself, and Luke chuckles silently, not missing a thing. Hmph.

Sulking, we sit there mutely for a few moments, overhearing snippets of the conversations around us, which consists either of food, hockey, or some crazy, hot chick. Their descriptor, not mine.

Glancing down at my phone, I note that we're making good time. But I better get in a few more questions while I still can. I clear my throat, ready to begin, when Luke rubs his forehead with a groan. He's obviously smart enough to know he's not off the hook yet. I look him up and down. He's strong. He can take a few more prods, I hope.

"So why pre-med? Don't most jocks choose business management or history?"

"We prefer the term student athletes."

"My bad," I say contritely. "But you still haven't answered my question."

"Which one? There have been dozens," he grumbles, shifting in his seat.

"If hockey is your future after college, why pick such a difficult subject like pre-med to study?"

Luke shakes his head as if I don't get it, which is fair because I don't. I can't see why anyone would go through all the trouble if their heart isn't even in it?

"The odds of playing hockey in college are 13 to 1. At an NCAA college like Thatcher, it's 41 to 1." Luke recites the figures as though it's something he calculates daily.

"Do you know the odds of going pro?" Luke asks, sounding like a teacher instructing a kindergartener, but I'm more fascinated than annoyed at his explanation, so I shake my head, wanting to hear more. "Around 7 percent," he confirms.

"Okay, but you beat those odds. You're already playing for an NCAA team and have NHL scouts and other agents interested too. You were also only one of twenty-five USA college players to compete in some big international conference in Belfast, Ireland last year where, naturally, you took home a gold medal. So, it's not like this is some unrealistic pipe dream. You *can* and most likely *will* go pro!"

"And then what?" he barks, shoving an agitated hand through his long, silky hair. "What if I'm injured? What if I'm stuck in the minors forever? And even if I make it, the average NHL career is around five years."

"But that's five years of doing what you love, at least," I say urgently. "My granny used to say that whatever you like to do is exactly what you're meant to be doing. You can figure out the hows and what ifs along the way."

Luke huffs. "I can't expect you to understand," he says, shaking his head. "You're all passion and teapots, but I live in the real world, not through some social media filtered one."

Triggered, I twist around and jab his brawny arm. "Puck you, too, then! Here I was about to thank you for calling me passionate. My bad for assuming *you* were too." Annoyed, I cross my arms and look out the window at the leafless trees streaking by. We're surprisingly hauling ass considering the size of this bus.

After a moment, Luke gruffly says, "Sorry." His breath tickles my ear again. When I don't answer, it's his elbow gently jabbing me this time, but I continue to keep my focus on the moving landscape. "You know," he says, sounding playful, "in comparison, only 1.7 percent of college soccer players end up playing professionally. Something your boy Diego needs to recognize."

"He's not my boy!" My head whips around, and by the smug smile spreading across Luke's face, I'm wondering if that was his intention.

Unfazed by my outburst, his grin remains. "That's about one in a gajillion-bazillion infinity. Good luck with that, D-Nasty."

I resist rising to his bait again, but it's not easy. Several responses spring to mind, but none seem good enough to spit back, and I already used the 'puck you' pun I'd been saving. Instead, I settle for tapping my foot, which looks like it's trying to stomp out in morse code what my mouth won't. Dammit.

Stewing, I try to concentrate on the behind-the-scenes footage I plan to capture at today's away game and the other stuff I need to do, but all I can think about is Luke's resoluteness. He's living a hockey lover's fantasy, yet willing to shelve his dreams. I shake my head and break the silence between us. "But you could always get your degree later."

Luke groans and shoves a hand into the pocket of his zip-up jacket, fetching out a crumpled travel eye mask. Ignoring me, he places the mask around his head and pulls it over his eyes.

I guess that's the end of the interview. With only twenty minutes left, I use the remaining time on the bus to review what Luke said, but more importantly, what he didn't.

8

JAX

Uм, who knew hockey was so intense and … sexy? And why didn't anyone clue me in sooner?

Everything about it is fast paced. In comparison, every other sport moves at a glacial pace. Here, something is always happening, and the second I stop recording or put down my phone, I seem to miss a play that's even better than the last.

Despite the other team having numerous conference and championship banners flying from their rafters, the two seem equally matched, except they don't appear to have a star player like Luke. And I'm not being biased. Yes, I'm obviously rooting for my college, but no. From what I'm witnessing, it's a fact.

I couldn't have asked for a better spot to watch the game too. I'm seated alongside Coach Tavish and the alternates on the away bench right next to the penalty box. Mr. Ice Man had a meltdown earlier when he found out I wasn't going to be in the stands, arguing that I'd be in the way and a distraction to the team. I don't know what he expects me to be doing that I'd be such a disruption. It's not like I'm about to do a one-woman flash mob. Nor do I have a whole camera rig with me. I'm just using my cell phone to capture footage.

I flinch when Luke smashes an opponent up against the glass so forcefully that the other guy's helmet flies off. No blood, thankfully, but a shiver skates over me anyway.

When Luke is sent to the "sin bin," he shoots me an agitated glance as if it's my fault that he's doing time. But once he sits down, his attention immediately snaps back to the action. His gaze follows the puck like a cat pursuing the red light of a laser pointer.

And I'm sitting here watching him watch. Geez. I tell myself to concentrate on the game and not Luke, but for some reason, my head doesn't want to cooperate. No matter because he's been released from the box and is back in the game. Without missing a beat, Luke is already in possession of the puck. It's as though the black disc is being sucked in by his magnetism as well.

There is no denying that every guy out on that ice is a lethal, skilled athlete, but there is something about the way Luke plays that draws every eye to him. At least, mine for sure are. I never got the whole football player obsession of some girls, but hockey? Now this is a sport I can get behind. And I'm eyeing Luke's "behind" like it's a limited-edition Gucci bag. The bulky padding can't hide his sinewy, powerful movements either. Yup, it's safe to say that during the three periods of my first Thunderblades' game, I became a fan girl. Just like that, I got hit with a Thatcher Thunderbolt!

It's the only explanation for why when Luke comes off the ice with a satisfied smile due to their 4 to 1 victory, I feel compelled to fling my arms around his neck and smack a quick congratulatory kiss on his lips.

I don't think, I just act. And now I'm literally dangling from his neck like a tacky garland of Mardi Gras beads. With the taste of Luke's salty lips still on mine, I come to my senses. Alarmed, I flick a nervous glance up at Luke's shocked, blue eyes, which aren't as cool or blasé as I remember them being.

"Congratulations," I say lamely. Releasing my hands, my body drags against his as I drop the last few inches to land back on my feet. When his gaze meets mine again, the punch of awareness between us is almost brutal.

"Thank you," Luke says gruffly, and I'm not sure if he's thanking me for the unexpected kiss or well wishes, but his deep voice practically has my bones melting, and I teeter on my feet. My body has never responded to someone's voice before, so I'm not sure why it is now.

And oh, my damn. I straight out kissed this man. No tongue, but I lingered. My lips are still tingling from the impact. How do I get past this? Should I smooch the rest of his teammates and pretend this is how I congratulate everyone? Hmm, I'm not exactly mad at the scenario. But … although I've been told more than once that I have a big pair of lady balls, I'm not *that* brave. Impulsive? Sure. Downright crazy? No. At least I wasn't until I was handed this assignment.

"You played great," I add, brushing off the moment even though it's the last thing I want to do. "I got it all here," I gush, holding up my phone as proof. I'm tempted to smack my forehead with it, though, for sounding like a mindless fan.

Luke opens his mouth to speak, but before he can respond, he is being pushed away in the stream of his celebrating teammates heading to the locker room.

"We'll see you on the bus in an hour," Coach Tavish says, slapping me on the back when he passes.

I guess it will be my turn to feign sleep later. Otherwise, it's going to be a long and embarrassing bus ride back to Thatcher College.

9

LUKE

WITH THE DEAFENING boos and cheers emanating from our common room, you'd think my housemates were watching the big game and not streaming last night's episode of *The Bachelor*. But our alternate captain and right defenseman Tyler Gagnon is a fan of the reality show, going so far as to create a bracket and take bets. I declined, even though the pool is looking deep.

Cal Chase, my freshman year roommate and an overall happy-go-lucky guy, has crashed the viewing party too. But instead of watching the show, he keeps asking me questions about Jax. Seems I can't escape her name even in my own house. Bad enough she's infiltrated my matches and has all my bros talking about her, now Cal as well. If I didn't know better, I'd think Cal was under Jax's mysterious spell too. But he's been hung up on his neighbor April since the start of our final year. Besides, his questions have been primarily focused on their communications projects.

Too bad Cal wasn't assigned to my team instead. That would have been a lot less complicated. For one thing, I wouldn't have the urge to kiss him every time we worked together. I shoot my buddy a glance to confirm my theory. Just as expected, nothing.

"Kick her out!" Tyler chants, shaking me out of the weird wormhole of thoughts I'd entered, all of which I blame on Jax. And the paperwork on my lap that is still not finished? Also Jax's fault.

Between thoughts of you know who, Cal's pestering for details, and the catty drama being spewed from the TV, I can't concentrate. So, I shove my laptop and books into my satchel and make to leave, but Diego, with a shit-eating grin, blocks my path. He managed to get a B minus on his film essay and now thinks he's Einstein. I bet Jax helped write the thing for him in the first place. Regardless, he's no longer on academic probation, so I can't chew him out for a change, and he knows it, thus the cocky-ass smirk plastered on his face the last couple of days.

Hell, I'd be smiling, too, if I could escape this place and make out with Jax whenever I wanted. The memory of her brief kiss flashes in my mind, and I suck on my lower lip, wishing it was hers. But then, I'd be the C student without a sports future, like Diego. No, no female distractions, especially not during the season. Not when everything has finally come to this—the Frost Conference, my MCAT exam, NHL draft, med school applications. I have a lot on my plate, and yet, here is Jax's fuck buddy, or whatever he is, adding to my stress.

"Where you off to, boss?" Diego asks as if he's the house president and not vice versa.

The last thing I want to do right now is deal with him, but he's not giving me a choice. "To The Cloister," I reply, slinging my satchel over my shoulder, hoping he'll step aside. In more ways than one.

"Afraid to stay and show us your sensitive side?" Diego asks, laughing at his own comment while showing off some neat footwork with a neon-yellow soccer ball that he's dribbling.

"Yeah, that must be it," I say flatly, but for some godforsaken reason, I don't leave it at that or push past him. No, I have to go and say, "Why are you hanging around here watching this crap? Shouldn't you be with your girlfriend now that you're off academic probation?"

Diego's smug smile intensifies, and I want to kick myself for revealing too much. Instead, I kick at the ball Diego has under his foot, but he easily recaptures it. "Jack? She's not my girlfriend," he says, and the tension instantly releases from my shoulders. I guess I didn't realize how much I needed for him to confirm this as well, but I no longer want to smash his face in or snatch the ball now bouncing off his knee. "Nah, we're through. She was too serious for me."

I choke on my own saliva. "Serious?" I guffaw. "She walks around campus in a teapot costume and changes majors more times than she does clothes for one of her fashion videos."

Diego laughs and hits me with a surprised look. "That's not the real Jack though. That's just her online persona. Otherwise, she mainly likes to make appearances at parties without really partying, hangs out with these boring, brainy girls, gets mad when I drink too much, and lectures harder than you did for putting off my paper till the last minute. Which is fine, whatever. Girls can be like that, but fuck, she never even let me get past second base."

I forcefully bite down to keep my jaw from dropping open. I'm tempted to ask how he defines his bases but am so relieved that he didn't score, I don't want to push my luck and ruin this insanely joyful feeling spreading through my veins. I mean, it's not like I care who Jax sleeps with, but Diego? No. Just no. Not him.

"Tough break," I tell him, grinning.

Diego nods and gives me a squinty stare as if he's trying to read my thoughts, and I don't like it. When he finally shuffles out of my way, I move for the exit, but he stops me when he says, "Dude, I know she's a thirst trap, but don't go freezing her, Ice Man."

Whatever the fuck that means. I nod, though, figuring this is his lame attempt at protecting her, and my opinion of the guy increases a measly notch. Not that I plan to do anything with Jax anyway. Even if I've thought about doing more, so what? Only natural that I've pictured it. I'm just an average, horny guy. End of story. It's not like I can't stop thinking about her, or that I've watched all her videos—even the one on how to cut up an oversize T-shirt so that it reveals her sexy shoulder on replay. Not like I listened to her scarf-tying tutorial, just so I could hear her voice before I went to bed last night. And if I did? Doesn't mean anything.

It can't because the only thing on my mind should be reviewing my sociology notes without disturbance, which is why I head to a secluded booth in the very back corner of The Cloister.

The student-run coffeehouse on upper campus is sort of a hideout for me on the rare afternoons I'm not in class or at practice. I like that it provides more background noise than the overly quiet library, plus the coffee is decent and it gets me out of the house.

Sliding into my favorite partially hidden booth, I check the clock on my phone. I should be able to study here without interruption for at least an hour before the space flips to an after-hours lounge. And according to the artfully decorated chalkboard up front, tonight is open mic night. I have no idea if it will be noisy or not, but I don't plan on sticking around to find out.

I haven't been to The Cloister's nighttime events since … well, damn. I guess not since Morgan and I were together. Her sorority had a fundraiser here with 10 percent of the proceeds and tips going to Theta Kappa Gamma Sorority. Thanks to the bikinis she and the other pledges were barely wearing, they raked in a lot of dough. When Morgan served me my plate, I remember joking that my salad had more dressing on than she did. Still personally proud of that cool line, but instead of being proud of her team, Morgan kept bragging how she'd earned the most.

I shake my head at the memory. If only being jealous and worrying about my social status were still my life's biggest problems. None of that shit even matters anymore, but still, recalling it has me annoyed—not at Morgan's vapidness, though, but at myself for getting caught up in her and Greek life. For wanting only that and hockey out of my college years, instead of preparing for the harsh realities of the real world like I was supposed to be doing all along.

Speaking of problems, Ms. Teapot is intently walking my way, her determined strides eating up the distance between us. Jax's hair moves about her wildly as if matching or competing with its owner's high energy. Due to her latest video, I now know the hair style is called "beach waves."

Still, why the hell my eyes rose intuitively to find hers across the room is beyond me. I guess it's what my childhood coach would call my "hockey sense," the mental side of the game. The ability to read the ice and read the play, but also to anticipate and understand where you and your teammates should be within an instant. I figure ever since Jax sort of joined our team, my senses have attuned to her in much the same way. Whatever the reason, it's damn inconvenient in this case.

"I thought I might find you here," Jax says with a genuine smile that lights up her face despite the early evening shadows that fill the room.

"Are you stalking me now?"

She doesn't seem to mind my tone or accusation. Instead, a small laugh bursts from her pouty lips. "Let's just say I have my spies."

I have no doubt her informant is Diego. My own fault for sharing where I was headed before storming out earlier.

Jax brazenly plops herself down on the same bench alongside where I'm working. Not that I mind, but given the fact that I chose this solitary corner, anyone else would have sat across from me or on the other side of the room even. But not Jax. Intoxicating, jasmine-scented Jax.

I scoot over in the booth, far enough to stop myself from touching her, but close enough to feel the heat of her. Our eyes meet, and my pulse and cock throb in time. Filling my lungs with air, I fight the impulse to lean Jax back and kiss a path down her exposed throat.

With a toss of her unruly, auburn hair, she picks up my opened textbook and flips it over so she can read the cover. For a second, she purses her lips in thought. "Professor Larkin likes to include questions related to the sidebar facts, so don't skip over those."

"Thanks," I tell her, snatching the book out of her hands. I don't know why I act like a schoolyard bully around her, but I can't help myself. It was either grab the book or pull her against me. My honed hockey sense selected the safer bet.

She searches my face, far too comfortable in her

intimate inspection when no one else finds me this approachable, at least not anymore. "Soooo, I don't know if you've caught wind of this yet, but campus gossip has us dating," she informs, laughing, but it comes out forced and kind of awkward, just like the subject matter.

Knowing full well that I'm likely responsible for that rumor, I hope the mock expression of shock I place on my face doesn't give me away. I don't feel guilty about it, though, since it was accidental on my part. And either way, it's for Jax's own good. If she only knew the crap the guys were saying in the locker room after our game the other day. Sure, it started off innocently enough with some of them saying she was sweet, but they weren't talking about the donuts she'd handed out on the bus.

I'm brought back to the present, when I notice that Jax's smile has faded. Her eyes are cast downward toward her lap, too, so I'm unable to read them. She picks at her nails for a second before speaking. "My ... uh ... overflow of emotion after your win is probably to blame," she says lifting her head, revealing sorrowful, puppy-dog eyes. "I'm really sorry about that kiss. I guess I got carried away with the excitement of the win and being at my first live hockey game and all. Honestly, I wasn't thinking, and I didn't mean for it to be a big deal."

The shake of my head is immediate. I sure as fuck don't want her regretting that kiss because it *was* a big deal for me. While it might have been chaste and unexpected, it'd been more rewarding than the W. For that brief second, I was transported back to my early days of playing for fun, without the pressure of tournaments and winning conferences. Besides, I don't think anyone really noticed our brief lip-lock anyway, and it's not the reason for the spreading rumors.

"Nah," I placate, "it's a tight-knit college. Someone

sneezes, and it gets written up in the alumni newsletter." She laughs at my statement, but her skeptical expression says she's not completely convinced. "Besides, if we're supposedly an item, at least now my team can focus on scoring out on the ice and not with you."

"Oh pahlease. I doubt they were even thinking that," she says, slapping my arm in censure.

I choke on the latte I'm sipping, and not because of her pitiful pat but from shock at how unaware she is. "Believe me, they were. After our game, I was pestered with dozens of Jack in the box references."

"Jack in the box?" she asks, wrinkling her pert nose in confusion, and it's adorable as hell. "Like the fast-food chain or the children's toy?"

The quizzical arch of her dark eyebrow tells me she's going to require more of an explanation. Fine. I don't like ratting on my bros, but she needs to be wary. We're all scum. The jerseys we wear are merely the equivalent of putting lipstick on pigs. "As in Cayden asking if I'd seen Jax's box yet. I said no, but similar innuendos continued from the rest of the group."

Instead of being affronted by the locker room talk, Jax emits an incredulous snort that is both dorky and somehow endearing. "All right, I get the reference now, but you said no, so then that settles it. I guess it will eventually blow over, and they'll see me as just one of the guys soon enough."

I roll my eyes at her naiveté and optimism. They will never see her as 'one of the guys' … not with her banging body and the direct way she looks at people, as if peering into their souls. "Just keep clear of the rookie Tanner," I tell her flatly, not bothering to elaborate how our newest teammate announced he'd like to jack off in her box. Or what happened next.

"The shy sophomore who was nursing a black eye on the bus ride home?" she questions with a sympathetic wince on his behalf.

I nod. "Yup, him."

"I thought the helmets and face guards would protect you guys from injuries like that."

"You'd think," I murmur vaguely, making a show of flipping through my notes instead of confessing that Tanner's injury occurred from my fist after the game and not from playing hockey. Sure, he was just trying to show off, but I figure I gave the rookie a free lesson in shutting the hell up next time. OK technically he's not a "rookie" anymore, but irregardless he hasn't proven himself yet.

Anyway, so yeah, I know perfectly well it was my act of macho protectiveness that sealed the deal on the gossip being circulated. But the pup needed to learn his place. You never steal the puck from another Thunderblades' player, especially if your captain is in possession of it. It goes beyond the bro code. It's a teammate truce. I might as well have branded Jax with my number 22 since the result is pretty much the same—she's off limits. None of my teammates even dared to look her way as she slept during our ride home.

Why would I even care if they hit on her or make lewd references behind her back? Well, that I'd rather not overanalyze. But I do know it will be better for the team and Jax's communications plan if they backed off. That's all.

"My point is, rumors were bound to happen, especially considering I haven't spent this much time with any girl here since Morgan." I'm not sure why I shared this detail, but too late. Jax only nods as she thinks it over and is silent as we both observe the Cloister staff setting up the stage for later.

"That's something else I can't figure out. You and Morgan," Jax says, jumping topics as usual. But it's her repulsed expression, like she ate something sour that has me releasing an unexpected bark of laughter, causing a passing student waitress to stop mid-stride.

Ignoring the glances our way, I give Jax a hapless shrug. "We were high school sweethearts; you know how those go."

"No, I don't," Jax says, furrowing her brows.

"Oh," I say, fumbling. "I guess I figured you'd have had one or twenty of those."

Jax chuckles as if what I said was hysterical, and I'm back to being confused as usual around her.

"Nope, what I *had* were braces and twenty extra pounds, definitely no sweethearts."

"Huh," I say for lack of anything better because glancing at the confident and beautiful woman next to me, it's hard to comprehend there was a time she wasn't. Besides, twenty pounds is nothing especially if it added to her lush curves. Nah, I'm not buying it. I bet she was still just as pretty and irritating several years ago too. The boys were probably too intimidated to make a move. I don't blame them.

"Were you two in luuuve?" Jax sings her obnoxious question like a teasing child, and I roll my eyes.

"Anyone ever tell you that you have no filter?"

"Yup, all the time," she confesses proudly. "So, were you?"

Resigned to her inquisition, I relax my shoulders and expound more than usual on the matter, but for some reason, it feels natural to share this with her. Jax has that way about her that invites you to lay it all on the line, to spill your heart and guts out, no matter the risk. And stupidly, I do. "I thought so, but we'd have made it beyond just the good times if it were real love."

"Hmm." Jax mumbles and purses her lips.

I force myself from divulging more despite the odd pull to do so, and it's so obvious that Jax is fighting an inward battle not to pry further. The effort must be killing her because she is anything if not curious by nature. But her temporary lapse has me wondering a few things too. "How about you? Ever been in love?" Yup, just another question I never thought I'd ask anyone, never mind someone I've known for such a short time.

"No," she says a little wistfully. "And I refuse to say those three words until I'm absolutely sure." To further her statement, she bobs her head with conviction.

"So, you're a romantic," I point out a little shocked, because if so, then why the hell was she even talking with D-Nasty?

"I don't know about that," she says, shaking her head. "I just think the declaration gets used a little too casually, if you ask me. My mom has been 'in love' more times than I can count, only to have each relationship fall apart, leaving her looking the fool. Or like you, in hindsight realizing it wasn't real love, but something else."

"And you don't want to make the same mistakes." It's not a question but a fact. And when Jax nods approvingly, a wave of validation rolls over me.

"She always stays at the party too long, my mother, which is why I believe if you're not 100 percent sure, it's best to leave before you get too comfortable and start mistaking lust for love."

Hmm, no wonder she broke it off with Diego before things progressed any further. I nod, beginning to understand this teapot better, and I'm shook by the revelation.

Silence stretches between us, but it isn't uncomfortable, strange as that is. Reaching across me, Jax opens my textbook again to where my napkin placeholder is, then closes it. "When I'm ready, I just want it to mean something when I say it," she adds, returning to the conversation, her fingers moving on to fidget with the band on her smartwatch. I doubt she's aware of either action, simply needing something to keep her hands occupied like her racing mind is.

"I respect that," I say with a nod. Hell, I get it too. I've learned that it's much, much easier to exist with ice for a heart. Although the way Jax does it seems risky, continually opening her heart up to be bruised, but then shutting it before it can break. Better to keep it permanently closed if you ask me. Clearing my throat I continue my train of thought, "That's why I've stayed clear of relationships for the time being. You know, outside of our supposed one," I add with a playful elbow nudge to her side to lighten the mood.

Jax chuckles briefly and bumps me back with a shove of her shoulder. "Hmm, you know," she says, dragging out her thought, a slow, mischievous smile tugging at her lips. "Everyone seems to think you and I are really together and … I suppose if I were truly your girlfriend, you couldn't very well complain about posing for the team calendar? Especially when it's so important to me and my grade and all."

She sends me a pleading look that tugs at me for a millisecond, but I tamper down its effect, shoving it away as I would an opponent. "Nice try," I tell her, both impressed and annoyed at her attempt to maneuver me, but she'll have to do better than that. There is no doubt I feel more than a slight pull of attraction for her, but been there, done that. "But you're not my girlfriend, so it's a hard no."

Her unexpected gasp is so loud that I straighten in surprise when more heads turn our way. "Are you breaking up with me?" she screeches, sounding like one of the deranged contestants on *The Bachelor*.

"Are you crazy?" I ask under my breath, but Jax only smiles wider. Her eyes light with mischief, and I can feel the bench beneath us shake with her quiet laughter.

"Crazy?" she echoes, only about ten times louder than is normal for any sane person. This time, more heads swivel to look at us, and I want to hide under the table because that hockey sense of mine is warning me it's going to get worse. "Crazy in love with you!"

Yup, knew it. Outside of the rink, I loathe attention, so I'm quick to reach over and cover her mouth with my hand, preventing her from casting an even bigger spotlight on us. "All right, you little brat, you win!" I hiss at her and feel her lush lips curve into a smile under my cupped hand. "Just be quiet."

She nods swiftly, eager to agree now that she got her way, confirming that she is, in fact, a brat. One whom I want to kiss. I slowly slip my hand away from her mouth, and for a second, I imagine doing just that before my brain takes over and I'm scooting safely away from temptation. Not that I can really escape completely in this tight booth with her on the end.

"You're kind of nuts, you know that?" I grumble, but she only agrees with another nod and a sweet grin. Grr!

"Aww, but that was our first fight, pookie," she says in a fake girly voice while batting her eyes rapidly. I can't help but give in and laugh at the absurdity of it all, and while people continue to stare, this time, I don't give it much thought. "You know," she continues with a teasing chuckle that has me both afraid yet eager to hear what she's going to come out with next, because really, anything goes with Jax. She better not declare we're engaged or that she's pregnant next. "This relationship," she says using air quotes and a side wink, "sure has been a whirlwind. But we've skipped all the good stuff though."

"More like fast forwarding through the bad," I say, picturing the couple of painful dates I had since Morgan. I mean, sure, I've hooked up with a few puck bunnies over the summer breaks and after the Belfast Tournament. What can I say? Scoring has always been easy for me on and off the ice, but the rest of the stuff that goes with it, not so much. Which is fine by me, because frankly, a woman for more than one night isn't worth the drama and complications. Especially not at this time in my life. I've done enough compromising for one lifetime.

I shake my head just thinking about dating. "None of that getting-to-know-you awkwardness, finding common ground, figuring out what to say, where to go …"

"Oh, but that's my favorite part!" she exclaims, squeezing my leg just above the knee. She's so taken with her romantic visions, I'm not sure she realizes she's doing it.

"Of course it is," I reply, not the least bit surprised that Jax, with five majors under her belt, wouldn't equally love the newness of relationships, too, then loving and leaving them fast. "So, this would be like what, our third date by now?" I ask, humoring her.

"At least," she says, sipping from my latte, and I don't even mind. If that's not a sign of a beaten-down boyfriend, then I don't know what is. Whoa! Why the fuck am I going along with this picture? We are not boyfriend and girlfriend; we're not anything. We're just … But I don't have time to reflect because naturally, Jax is talking again.

"Then again, by the third date, we'd have hooked up more than just that little smooch though."

My ears seem to perk up on their own, clearly liking the sound of where she might be going with this. Her tone is no longer teasing either. It's … it's flirtatious. "You're right," I say, my gaze narrowing in on her glossy, bubblegum-colored lips. Before I can talk myself out of it, I'm leaning in to taste them. It's just a silly game, no harm, no foul. A kiss never derailed anyone.

Wrong! Kissing Jax, I mean, truly kissing her like I'm doing now? Feasting on her lips and swallowing her little moans are enough to have me fisting a handful of her thick hair and grinding her face closer to mine. Her mouth is so full and so much more intoxicating than I was expecting. It's as if our lips are starved for one another, eager to finish what was barely started the other day. Our tongues battle for control, and I can't tell who is winning the fight. All I know is that I want this. No, I want more. More. The word is chanting inside my frantic brain.

As if reading my mind, Jax throws a tight, jean-clad leg over mine and shifts so she's sitting astride my lap with her back resting up against the table's edge behind her. Straightaway, my right hand leaves its grip on her tangled mane to clutch her fine ass. Fuck! One ripe cheek fits perfectly in my large palm as if it was made for me to scoop it. To cup it. But she's not nearly close enough to quench the fiery desire within me, especially when she rocks forward and tugs on the ends of my hair, all the while sucking and pulling at my lips. The blood is roaring in my ears, and I can't hold on to a single thought. Every worry or concern is obliterated by my need for her. This addictive and unpredictable woman.

With a sexy exhale, Jax's body melts under my insatiable touch. Her breasts crash into my chest, and my dick leaps with excitement. I can't seem to stop feeling her, and my other hand rubs up and down her back, mashing her boobs farther into me, hoping to absorb every ounce of her.

I can skate and do drills for hours without panting, but one brain-numbing kiss from Jax and my heart is racing to the point where I'm worried for my health. It's not until she briefly breaks for air that I realize what I'm doing and where we're doing it. Regrettably, I release my hold, and Jax falls back against the table, her hair spilling forward in abandon. She's even more beautiful with her lips swollen and her appearance mussed. From my doing. Lord, help me. Images of her like this in my bed naked swarm my brain.

With a shaky hand, Jax smooths back her wild hair. But her chest continues to rise and fall with her deep breaths, and the enticing sight does nothing to control my raging lust. Not to mention, she's still straddling me, and I'm harder than I've ever been in my fucking life. If it wasn't for the denim separating us, I'd be in absolute heaven right now.

"What's wrong?" Jax questions, sounding dazed, her hazel eyes glassy in confusion.

"Wrong?" I croak, but it comes out so deep and serious that I barely recognize the voice as my own. I clear my throat and fight for some semblance of sensible thought. "I almost took you right here on this bench, woman!"

The devilish glint in her eyes and lopsided smirk tell me I said the wrong thing. "That wasn't supposed to turn you on," I amend with a groan, dropping my head and letting it fall on her shoulder.

"Too late," she answers with a throaty chuckle that vibrates through our tangled bodies, and I shake my head into the nook of her warm, jasmine-scented neck and breathe her in. Too late is right.

Pushing back, I take Jax in once more and contemplate carrying her out of here and back to my place. "What am I going to do with you?"

With the sexiest fucking smile that I've ever seen in my life, Jax has the nerve to say, "More of that, please! Oh, definitely more of that."

It's on the tip of my tongue to admit she could have anything she wants, but the unsolicited thought scares me more than the upcoming draft and MCAT exam combined. I've been down this road before and took careful steps to ensure that I'd never be back. But then again, I never planned on Jax.

Looking more alert now, Jax slips off my lap, and the loss of her heat and pressure has me groaning. I immediately want to pull her back, but I control myself. Casting a worried glance around the room, Jax does a double take when she encounters something or someone near the entrance.

Concerned, I narrow in on what she's looking at, but I only see two female students selecting a high-top table toward the resurrected stage. One girl is a tall glass of water and the other is a shot glass. The former I recognize as a shy junior from last year's chemistry course who always sat in the front row and was quick to answer the professor's questions. I wanna say her name is Emerson, and she's talking to the petite April Harris, a.k.a. Cal Chase's gal. She just doesn't know it yet.

"I gotta go," Jax whispers as if her friends will overhear from across the room. "I'll see you Friday in the auditorium. I'll text you the details, but don't worry about what to wear. We'll outfit you there. Or rather, de-outfit you," Jax says, biting back a laugh.

I'm about to argue now that the blood has finally returned north to my brain, but Jax silences me with a quick goodbye peck on the lips. And for reasons I can't fathom, it feels like we've shared the intimacy hundreds of times before. Jax smiles in equal wonder and then slinks out through the back exit before I can say another word.

I swear, she never fails to keep me guessing, and for someone who craves order and predictability, I have no idea why I'm smirking from ear to ear.

10

JAX

"No, no," I assure Emerson, who is crinkling her brow in worry when we pop a squat in between classes on a bench alongside April. It's cold outside, but not so bad considering it is November.

Once again, I shake my head in denial. "It was nothing!"

Nothing except the best bone-melting kiss of my life. Alright, okay, so maybe it's something, but it's definitely not defined. Whether it's the start of something or just a rumor that we got carried away with, I have no idea.

"But—" Emerson begins to sputter.

"A few kisses does not a relationship make," April interjects poetically for me.

"Exactly!" I say, nodding, happy she at least gets it.

"I should know," April mumbles under her breath, and neither Emerson nor I comment on that part. April is not someone you can push. She'll share more when and only when she wants to, and we'll both be there for her when she does.

But back to my kisses. Defined or not, I'm enjoying

simply being around Luke, and I grow warm just thinking about what happened yesterday in The Cloister, of all places!

"Uh-oh," Emerson says, wagging a finger in front of my face. "Check out that goofy grin. You look like you're up floating around cloud nine."

Wrong. Since the impromptu make-out session with Luke, I'd have to look down to see cloud nine. And twice, I've been busted for humming without even realizing it. I can only imagine how silly I'd be acting if we were really dating. Instead of scaring me like relationships typically do, the idea makes me smile.

"She's right," April adds with a firm nod. "You're looking like one of your lovesick guys. Guess the tables have turned."

My smile fades faster than dollar-store lipstick. Love? If it were truly more, I'd know it, right? It's just the newness of a crush, that's all. And I love new. "No way!" I exclaim with an assuredness I don't feel, and my so-called friends are now laughing at my expense.

Before I can begin to build my defense, Cal Chase runs past our bench, then doubles back after spotting us, or more likely, April. He's dressed in his team track shorts and matching tank, and I do an involuntary shiver imagining how freezing I'd be if I were wearing that outside today. He's glistening with sweat, though, and doesn't seem the least bit bothered by the brisk air.

"Hello," he says with a charming smile, throwing a hand quickly through his chocolate-brown hair. "The three of you together are enough to make a guy trip and fall on his face."

"Promises, promises," April says with a scowl, and I fight to hold in my gasp at her rudeness, but Cal only laughs.

"How's your coms project going, Jax?" he asks, briefly looking at me before darting his gaze back at April, who has her head turned determinedly away.

"So far so good. How about yours?"

"I'm jogging over to the crosswalk now," he says with a nod. "Sounds like you've really hit it off with my pal Luke, huh?"

That's right, they're friends, even though they couldn't be more opposite. Interesting. "He's just my point of contact for the Thunderblades." I give what I hope is a dismissive shrug because you know, hit it off, make out, sit on his lap, same thing. Fix your face, Jax, before it gets all dreamy again!

Cal bobs his head innocently, but his expression isn't. "But I mean, like, on a personal level, you two seem to be getting along ..." he trails off, fishing for more details. Geez, he's just as bad as my girls.

"Yeah, I guess so. He's a funny guy and surprisingly easy to be with," I babble, not sure what I'm even saying thanks to three pairs of prying eyes aimed at me. I refrain from adding that there's also a quiet intensity to Luke that draws you in.

Cal bursts out laughing while rubbing his slight beard, if you can even call it that since it's so trimmed. Just enough scruff on his jaw to give him a tough but lovable look. "There are many terms I'd use to describe Luke, but 'funny' isn't one of them."

His observation leaves me bristling inside and feeling defensive. "Maybe witty is more accurate," I admit, recalling the times Luke has made me laugh with a quick comeback or simply because he tries so hard to be serious all the time, which I find laughable. I especially relish when I'm able to make Luke chuckle in return and chip away at the ice wall he likes to have up around him.

"Hey, don't get me wrong, love the guy, but he's as serious as a heart attack. You can't really blame him for that though. He hasn't had it easy the last few years," Cal supplies with an empathetic countenance set on his handsome face.

I lean in closer. "What do you mean?"

A voice deeper and smokier than Cal's breaks into our foursome. "Excuse me, is this exhibitionist bothering you ladies?"

"Steel!" Emerson exclaims, lighting up brighter than Times Square, and Steel shoots her a wink. I've never seen Em act this way, and it's cute to witness.

"Thought I might find you here," Steel says, lifting a cardboard carton with four to-go cups nestled inside. "Brought you all some hot cocoa," he says and passes one to Emerson and another to me, infusing heat instantly into my palms. "And one for June bug," Steel adds, extending a cup out to April, who naturally beams at the latest nickname he's come up with. She's more than a tad obsessed with her first name, and Steel is the only one who indulges our friend by calling her different months and seasons.

"Sorry, dude," Steel says, turning to Cal, who was watching their exchange through narrowed eyes. "I would have gotten you one if I'd known. Here, you can have mine."

"No worries, I still have two more miles to go," Cal says, lifting a fist, and the two of them do some sort of guy greeting that looks more like the start of a game of rock, paper, scissors.

"How cute. You two have your own secret handshake," April teases.

"Jealous?" Cal asks, sounding more hopeful than mocking, but when April shakes her head, sending her short, bob haircut swishing back and forth, Cal's happy-go-lucky expression falls. The poor dude really needs to pull back and let April come to him. She will eventually. At least, I hope so because I'm rooting for the guy, but I can't intervene too much, either, or she'll retreat even more.

"Gotta run," Cal says before literally doing so. "Later, Thisbe," he calls over his shoulder. Emerson and I look around, not sure who he was referring to, but April merely purses her lips, leaving us to assume it's some inside reference between the two. That's a good sign, right?

Meanwhile, now that Steel has joined us, I seize the opportunity to ask him something. "Steel?" I question, and he politely turns his attention away from Emerson. His dark head bobs, waiting for me to go on, and I continue before I lose my nerve. "Would you consider maybe singing the anthem at an upcoming Thunderblades' home game?"

Emerson kicks me in the shin and shoots me a glare while Steel mulls it over. I give my friend a pleading look in return. It's not like I'm relishing putting Steel in an awkward position, but the internship program tops any personal embarrassment. And I couldn't very well leave it up to Emerson to ask because I know she wouldn't have dared to.

"Don't you mean my dad?" Steel replies coolly, his stormy eyes blazing with annoyance.

I shake my head. "No, *you*. Emerson was just saying how great your performance was at The Cloister last night."

Steel's face softens. "Sure, why not?" he eventually says with a smile, and I hear Emerson release a whoosh of air. "As long as you three are there to watch," he adds, but although he said three, his eyes remain focused on only one —Emerson.

"Thank you, thank you!" I gush, already putting together a mental list of next steps. Yes, yes, yes!

Steel flips his wrist to check the time on his expensive-looking watch. The motion reveals a sexy guitar pick tattoo on the inside of his wrist too. It's not as big as Luke's 22 though. Hmm. Guess I'm developing a tat fetish as of late. Maybe I should get one! No, I'd never be able to settle on just one and would probably end up looking like a cluttered chalkboard you can't erase.

"Lab starts in twenty," Steel states, his gray eyes still set possessively on Emerson. "And I know how you like to be there early, Em. Ready, partner?"

I'll go ahead and assume Steel didn't mean to sound like a cowboy there, but I guess they *are* partners this semester for Advanced Bio, so I bite my tongue. Initially, Emerson wasn't happy about being teamed up with him, but looks like she's changed her mind. She's standing before he can even finish his question, and they both stroll down the same path as Cal did, sipping their hot chocolates and stealing glances at one another.

"And then there were two," April says solemnly with a shake of her head.

Laughing, I throw an arm around her shoulders and give her a playful squeeze. What can I say? I love this little grump. "Cheer up. At least we get perks like cocoa, and hey, I think he knows Taylor Swift."

April only nods, which might as well be an open invitation for me to push harder to crack her mood. "Shake it off. Shake it off," I sing, doing a terrible Swifty impression, but it does the trick, and April laughs begrudgingly. And when we get up to leave, April is humming another Taylor tune.

11

LUKE

I COME to an abrupt stop after entering the auditorium Friday. I'm too dumbstruck over the juxtaposition of what looks like a rinky-dink school play crossed with a porno scene.

My teammates are scattered about the theater stage, bare-chested and flexing. Cayden Morell has his number 11 painted in red over his washboard abs, Blake is brandishing his hockey stick like it's a lightsaber, and our big, gruff defenseman Tyler is holding up an entire bench over his head as a photographer calls out compliments and snaps his camera.

"There you are," Tanner shouts over the chaos. I hadn't noticed him in the back with just his helmet and shorts on, balancing a puck on his bicep, and frankly, I wish I hadn't seen him like that at all. "We already did our individual shots, but you're just in time for the group cover."

Ignoring him, I start to back out the door when Jax's voice calls out, "Come on, Ice Man, don't be afraid," laughter evident in her voice as she draws closer. I'm about to tell her she has enough man flesh to fill the calendar without me, but her voice does things to me. Like agreeing to pose for this ridiculous calendar. I will myself to leave, but when she hooks her arm through mine and says, "Do it for the team," I'm good and captured.

Just great. How many times have I heard that directive lately? I'm not sure if it's the be-a-team-player edict or maybe her touch, but I let her pull me forward and lead me toward the stage like a show pony. Some of the guys have the nerve to clap. I'm so getting them back at practice tomorrow. Extra strides for sure, starting with the blue line and back, followed by the red line, and the far goal line. Ha! That will keep these guys in check and remind them why we skate, which has nothing to do with the fawning fans who will buy these calendars. For love of the game, not fame.

Standing in front of me, Jax leans up on her tiptoes and pulls off my baseball cap, causing my hair to fall forward. Biting her plump bottom lip, she runs her hands through the strands to sooth away my hat hair, and damn if the way her nails gently scratch my scalp doesn't have me wanting to purr like a cat.

"I'm getting you back for this too," I manage through gritted teeth.

Her amber eyes grow in alarm. "Me?" she asks innocently, too innocently.

I nod toward the rest of the guys. "Yes, you and your lap dogs."

She laughs and pats my head. "Now, be a good puppy and do this one little trick for me, okay?"

"You're pushing it," I warn her, but Jax only nods in agreement, as usual.

With a slight blush coloring her cheeks, she slides off my vintage NHL bomber jacket and her hands brush my chest in more of a caress than is necessary for the action. My skin heats up wherever she touches, and goose bumps break out on my forearms. Through hooded eyes, I glance down at her, but I can only see the top of her head since her gaze is fixated on the waistband of my athletic joggers. "Oh, no," I groan.

Her own voice is husky when she answers. "These can stay on since they're Thatcher scarlet, but this—" She reaches for the hem of my T-shirt, and I'm no longer anti-undressing now that Jax is the one doing it for me.

"Can we hurry it up?" a male voice belonging to the photographer shouts, and I leap back from Jax's raised hands. "I have my own work to do today, too, you know? Lose the shirt, big guy, grab a prop from the bin, and join your team."

"For the team," I mutter and climb the three steps to stand on the stage. Peeling off my T-shirt myself, I throw it down to Jax, who neatly insides it out and places it with my jacket on the first row of seats. After which, she has the nerve to sit there cross-legged as if she's taking in a show, but I guess she is. The only prop left is a corny, inflatable lightning bolt, but I grab it, thankful I'm not stuck with a dorky foam finger like our goalie.

Click! Click! Click!

"Yo, Captain," the school's yearbook photographer yells, his dark eyes fixated on his viewfinder. I believe his name is Asif, and although I've seen the guy before, it's the first time I'm seeing the new stache he's wearing, which is a cross between a handlebar and I don't know what. Maybe he grew it in for Movemeber? A few of us did the challenge freshman year, but we looked more like Gomez Adams than Tom Selleck.

"Do you think you could possibly *not* look like a deer in headlights?" Asif asks, still not bothering to look up from his camera. Grr! I plaster on a smile, but he quickly tells me to lose it. "No, no, go back to brooding." Easy enough, considering I want to get the hell out of here as soon as possible. "Um, now you just look constipated," Asif declares, and the team breaks out into a chorus of sniggers.

"I'm outta here," I protest, and I'm sure the look I'm now delivering is more murderous than sexy.

"Chill, babe," Asif cajoles. "Give me bedroom eyes." More laughing is triggered. "Imagine the last person you hooked up with. Picture that encounter."

Just like it has done repeatedly over the last few days, images of Jax straddling me in The Cloister, her full tits pressed up against my chest, and my hands cupping her ass fill my brain. Shifting my head, I seek out the amber eyes haunting my dreams. My gaze tracks down Jax, and her mouth falls open. I continue to stare at her, now picturing all the things we haven't done.

"Yes, perfect! My camera is on fire."

It might be my oversexed imagination, but I think I hear Jax emit a little whimper from thirty feet away. Unable to break the invisible, tension-filled line that leads to Jax and back, I force myself to at least tone down my thoughts or the Thunderblades' calendar is going to go from PG-13 to X-rated quick. Thankfully, Asif moves his focus to picking on Tanner, diffusing the hunger building in me.

A few more snaps of his camera later, Asif is dismissing the rest of the team but tells me to put on a scarf and lean against a stack of fake, box-size ice cubes resembling an igloo totem pole for my solo shot.

I lumber over to the scene, throwing the stupid, plastic, blow-up bolt at Cayden, when he reminds me to not forget my bedroom eyes again before he wisely leaves.

While I assume my position as directed, Jax is busy

thanking everyone and delivering assurances that she'll see them at the Theta Sorority party later tonight. "They said you won't have to pay the usual cover fee." This news gets a few cheers out of the guys.

As the most popular sorority on campus, Morgan's TGIF parties are a weekly social staple to celebrate any Thatcher team wins, along with raising money for charity. Mostly, the football and soccer players head there after victories, but given my history with Morgan, my crew usually celebrates at another Greek house. And although Morgan's made it clear the invitation applies to us, too, I haven't been since my dumb hazing days.

Scowling, I picture Jax in Theta's crowded hall surrounded by a bunch of punk guys like Diego. Hmm … maybe it's past the time I make an appearance too. This way, I can be sure my team doesn't overdo it. It's the only responsible thing to do.

"Now don't look so grumpy, honey," Asif instructs, and I snap back to what I'm supposed to be doing—being a beefcake. Great. "Fold your arms across your chest, yes, like that, and throw me a cocky grin. I mean, throw your girl one." He inclines his head toward Jax and moves his camera stand closer.

"She's not my—" I say, not able to finish the denial. Don't want to.

Ignoring my faltering protest, Asif calls over his shoulder, "Jax, babe, come up here for a second!"

Dutifully, she heads our way with a smile. Standing a few feet away, she eyes me up and down. Unaware of the danger she's putting herself in, she comes closer and adjusts my scarf, then tugs on my pants so they sit lower on my hips. Seriously, I can't wait for payback, and a growl reverberates from my chest. My warning only makes her smile though. Of course it does.

"Come on, Ice, show me what you got," she dares again, her eyes glittering.

That's it! I drop my crossed arms and snag her hand before she can fully return to stand behind the camera. Tugging her fingers, I haul her up against my naked chest, and she lets out a tiny squeak.

"Happy to," I say, lifting her chin and capturing her parted lips with mine.

Instantly, the teasing kiss turns to wildfire, just like Jax herself. Eagerly, almost frantic, our tongues find each other, our air coming in shorter supply. Her nails dig into my shoulders. God, this woman! She's all but climbing me to get closer, and I'm a second away from breaking all my rules and scooping her up and …

It takes Asif's clearing of his throat to break us apart. This time, Jax jumps guiltily away.

"Ready?" Asif asks, sounding bored to tears.

Ready for a cold shower is more like it. I nod, and Asif seizes the moment, shooting off several shots on burst while I stare down Jax like she's a puck in a shoot-out. A puck I'd like to fuck, that is.

Yup, I'm totally pucked!

12

JAX

I ᴋɴᴏᴡ the instant Luke walks into Theta Kappa Gamma house later that night.

My Luke-tuned senses on high alert, I turn around just as he strolls in, my heart racing at the mere sight of him. I smile, oddly happy to see him, even if he looks grumpy, as usual. His arrival is an hour after everyone else, but I hadn't expected him to join the party at all, and I'd be lying if I said that I wasn't happy he finally did.

"Happy" is an understatement. It's rather like I drank my weight in caffeine and am about to burst out of my skin. Overcome, I release a little sigh like a kid with a celebrity crush. Yup, a few of his kisses, and I've turned into a pathetic marshmallow. As long as I don't get roasted like a smore, I'm determined to ride it out and see where this thing goes. Maybe to my bed, my heart? Or nowhere. One way to find out.

Tucked out of sight near the entrance to the kitchen, I look my fill at Luke while Tanner drones on about his rookie-setting record as a defenseman last year. I already agreed to feature him in the next player spotlight video hoping that would shut him up, but it only seemed to spur his bragging. The only thing interesting I've learned so far is that he's Canadian, hailing from Montreal, and majoring in French. The hockey stats he seemed so proud of though, were just gibberish to me. I don't know what's wrong with me tonight, Tanner is cute and seems like a genuinely nice guy, but I can't muster my usual flirting. Not that he seems to notice and thanks to the booming music and a round of Jaeger shots, I've managed to drown him out to the point where he sounds like the adults in a *Peanuts* cartoon. Blah, blah, blah.

Across the room, confident and cool, but not cocky, Luke tucks a hand into the pocket of his hip-hugging jeans and takes another step into the crowd. Although, he'd have every right to be cocky considering he's a triple threat—a star athlete, handsome, *and* smart. He's also kind of sweet once you get past his frosty front. I bite back a smile after noticing he is wearing his usual look of annoyance. Now that I know him a little better, I appreciate that he doesn't bother with a fake smile like most guys on the prowl here tonight.

Weaving in between the crush of people, Luke stands a foot higher than most. He nods to a few of his teammates, who slap him on the shoulder as he passes. And I swear it's not my jealous imagination when I say that literally every girl tries to grab his attention along the way. How can I blame them? What a sight he is—his ass in those jeans is nothing shy of perfect, plus those full, pillowy lips and the way his hair hangs … well, it practically invites hands to reach out and touch it. To see if it's as silky as it looks, and boy is it. That I remember, among other parts of him that I had the pleasure to touch so far. And now, thanks to today's calendar shoot, I know exactly how jaw-dropping ripped he is too.

Luke stops his progression to observe Cal and April bantering or fighting. It's hard to know at this point. It's because of April and her ridiculous hookup plan that I'm here tonight. In the past, I've gained entrance to Theta's cliquish parties as Diego's guest, but since neither April nor I are sorority sisters, I had to promise I'd extend an invitation to the hockey team too. It was that or no entry because it's common knowledge that Morgan insists on her sisters being the only females to shine. Thus, why men outnumber the women here tonight and every night.

It's like infiltrating the queen's court. At least, that's what April pointed out in an impressive British accent when we arrived earlier. The male-to-female ratio is probably why poor Cal looks out of his mind with jealousy, especially with April looking like a bite-size snack in the purple, thigh-high dress she borrowed from my recent fashion pull. Going along with her asinine plan, I can only hope April makes out with someone else already and gets it over with. Then, she'll surely realize that Cal is the real deal and not a player hell-bent on annoying her.

Still standing ringside to the two heated lovebirds, Luke's blue eyes scan the crowd, eventually stopping when they encounter mine, and I choke on my drink. Then again, the alcohol inside it is so strong and menthol tasting that I probably would have choked no matter what. But I know damn well it's not the drink causing me to suck in air; it's the intangible heat between us.

"Easy, killer," Tanner says with a laugh when I stop coughing, and then leaves to refill my Solo cup without asking. I'm glad he's gone, so I don't bother to stop him even though I've had enough. Swiveling my head from Tanner's retreating back, I unabashedly track down Luke again and start when I see he's purposefully heading my way with his eyes narrowed slightly. Guilt fills my gut, which is stupid because I haven't done anything wrong being here or talking to Tanner. No doubt Luke blames me for bringing his team out tonight. Tough … besties over testies!

I nod indifferently when he stops in front of me, and the big brute does the same, neither of us seeming to want to admit defeat and speak first, which is ridiculous since this isn't a competition. Oh, but I have all night, pal! I smirk, and a faint smile tugs at his kissable, soft, cushiony lips. Remembering the feel of them almost has me moaning.

The air crackles between the two of us, but still, we say nothing as we stare each other down. His cool gaze shifts slowly down my body, causing a tingling awareness of heat on my skin. I'm rocking a red, bodycon bandage dress that I know shows off the twins and my booty, not that he's had a chance to see the back yet. Just wait, Ice Man! When his eyes meet mine again, they are no longer cool but on fire. Delight fills me at the desire I see pooled there.

Crossing his arms, Luke leans on the doorframe next to me. Very next to me. I desperately want to tackle him and ease the tension building inside me. Like legit tackle him, right here at this party, and have him beg to be let up. The pull is so fierce, a shiver runs down my spine.

Who am I kidding? I'm always the one who talks first. Dammit!

"Hi," I croak out. "I didn't think you'd come." I regret saying the word "come" the second it escapes my lips, and Luke's arched eyebrow only proves that he heard how my voice hitched too.

"Here's another drink, m'lady," Tanner interrupts, thrusting the red cup back into my hands, preventing me from hearing whatever Luke was about to finally say.

The two cut each other cock-measuring glances, both

standing up straighter as they do so. I roll my eyes, but not that either are looking at me to notice. Whatever. I down the drink and place it on the counter inside the kitchen. Yikes! I've had 100 percent moonshine that's gone down smoother than whatever Tanner poured. When I turn back, Luke's gaze is on the discarded cup.

"Hey, rookie, grab me whatever she's having," Luke orders. Good. I can't wait to see what Luke thinks of Tanner's bartending skills. With a fervent nod, Tanner scrambles to do Luke's bidding, like an eager subject pleasing his master. I guess that makes Luke two for two, winning both their posturing contest and our silent standoff. My mind might be a bit cloudy, but I'm thinking I wouldn't mind losing for a change. Not to him.

"I have no idea why you'd be surprised that I'm here," Luke drawls out, dropping his arm to his side. He then shakes his head as if he's annoyed at himself and not me for a change. "You got me doing TikToks, craving donuts, posing for a calendar"—he lists each offense, pausing a second before leaning his clean shaven face closer to mine with a glower—"kissing you instead of studying."

His exhale tickles the side of my neck, and it's not a shiver but an earthquake that races down my spine this time. "And the last part is *my* fault?" I manage, pointing a finger at my chest.

Luke nods, and I want to grab a fistful of his hair and drag his mouth to mine, which would only be proving his point, but who the fuck cares? If losing feels this good, he can win again and again.

"You look beautiful, Jax," Luke says huskily, his intense gaze eating me up. My heart thunders in my chest. He thinks I'm beautiful? The way he lingered on my name, too, which was way longer than three letters should take, has my bones melting. Luke opens his mouth to speak further, and I'm hanging on his every word, but again, he's cut off. This time by a feminine voice that could rival an angel.

"Look who's back among the living," Morgan Hyatt declares, familiarly wrapping an arm around Luke's waist. She places her back to me, effectively blocking me out.

Without much choice, I'm forced to take a step back and stare. Ugh, just lovely. They look like stereotypical Barbie and hockey Ken! To make matters worse, it's as if a spotlight is shining down on their perfection, and I shake my head to clear the image—the effects from the alcohol I've consumed, no doubt. I will myself to regain the confidence I'd felt earlier when I entered the party, or when Luke's ice-blue eyes had turned to fire when he looked me over. I might not be Barbie, but I'm no longer the ignored loner from high school, either, so I stand taller.

There is a tap on my shoulder, and I spin around, already annoyed at whoever is keeping me from the show. It's not Tanner, either, but April, and I soften my expression.

"Hey, do you know where Cal is?" she rushes to ask, her eyes wide with concern.

I shake my head. "No. The last time I saw him, he was with you. But at least you know where he lives."

She nods and turns to leave, but then pivots back. "Sorry. Do you mind if I ditch you?"

I laugh and gently push her toward the door. "Go! I'm a big girl, I'll be fine. Besides, I have some business to attend to."

And that business's name is Luke of Ice Enterprises.

13

LUKE

Jax's spine stiffens slightly, and accusing eyes meet mine over Morgan's head. I don't blame her. I'm just as shocked to have Morgan up against me and not Jax, like I was picturing only a second ago. What I'd wanted to do the moment I saw Jax standing over in this alcove tonight talking to Tanner—squeeze her up and absorb every ounce of her infectious joy for life and make her puny glare disappear.

Instead, having Morgan clinging to me is like having a bucket of Gatorade poured over my head. And it's not as fun as the commercials or ESPN make it look. No, it's sticky and cold, just like Morgan's hand biting into my hip. Still, unbidden memories flood my mind remembering the former us. Some things are better left in the past, though, and I shove away the nostalgic images temporarily fogging my brain.

Peeling off Morgan's bony arm, I break the embrace, mindful of the gossipy stares aimed our way. This isn't a stupid reality show, and I bristle over the fact that everyone is watching our dreaded reunion.

"I'm really glad you got *my* invite," Morgan declares, effectively rewriting the scene in her head, as usual. "It's so good to have you back at one of my TGIF parties again."

I might be at Morgan's party, but I'm sure as hell not here for her. "I couldn't miss it after Jax asked me to come." My turn to put the emphasis on "come." Grinning, I deliberately extend my hand past Morgan, hoping to hell my teapot won't scald me.

She does, but not in the way I feared. Jax's delicate hand curls into my palm, filling it with warmth the second I encompass it. With a slight squeeze, I tug her to my side, and as expected, she fits perfectly under my shoulder. Now, that's better.

Morgan's sharp, blue-green eyes take in the two of us, darting from my face to Jax's. "The rumors are true?" she asks, sounding both baffled and insulted.

"Yup," I say, holding Jax closer, silently urging her to play along. For once, Jax doesn't argue or talk, thank the hockey gods.

Morgan shifts her full attention to Jax, scornfully looking her up and down. So help me, I'm about to lay into her, but Morgan gets in the first passive-aggressive punch. Unfortunately, Jax is her target.

"That's such a stunning dress," Morgan says pleasantly. "But I guess you must really love it, too, since you've worn it to two of my parties now. Aren't you supposed to be like a fashion influencer?"

Several hovering girls snigger at Morgan's letdown, but Jax only snorts with amusement. Meanwhile, my teeth are mashing together so hard I can taste blood.

"Thank you, Morgs. So sweet of you to keep tabs on my wardrobe," Jax responds, mimicking Morgan's nice-on-the-surface voice to perfection. "You see, I believe in sustainability and quality over quantity."

Morgan scoffs and inclines her head toward me. "Yes, evidently you *do* like to reuse things."

My brain is telling me not to say shit, to just let it go. It's not worth it. But my mouth … "Careful, Morgan," I warn, but she ignores me.

Protectively, I bring Jax closer to my side. Morgan's backhanded compliments are nothing new to me, but picking on Jax is another story. Hell, if she were anyone else—a competitor on the ice—Morgan would be on her ass by now.

"Oh, and I've been meaning to tell you how much I love your all-natural look," Morgan adds, aiming unkind eyes back at Jax. "It must take a lot of guts to not wear makeup, especially when you only have your assets to work with, that is."

"Well, my greatest asset is my personality. Maybe you should get one!"

I almost laugh out loud at Jax's comeback, but hold it in, masking my features. My laughter will only spark Morgan's venom further and while Jax might not need me to fight her battles, I don't want to add fuel to the fire either. However, the crowd's amusement has Morgan's face heating just the same. She flashes a menacing glare over her shoulder and immediately the onlookers disperse, eagerly heading to refill their drinks or to say hello to some long-lost friend.

Through a strained smile, Morgan lowers her voice to a hiss in my direction. "When you were finally ready to live again, I assumed you'd come back to me."

You assumed wrong is what I'd like to say, but I clamp down the urge, not wanting to completely stoop to her level. Still, I can't even fathom how she could think this way after all this time. "It's been three years, Morgan," I say, pointing out the obvious with a resigned sigh.

"I know," Morgan bites back between clenched teeth, still appearing to be smiling to anyone who might dare glance our way again. "Three long years waiting for you to come to your senses instead of digging yourself a grave next to your dear mother."

Under my arm, Jax turns as rigid as a board, shock registering with a soft whoosh of air releasing from her lips. I can sense her staring up at me, but I can't bring myself to confirm it, not here, not now.

With an even faker smile than before, Morgan neatly flips her perfectly styled hair over one shoulder as though she didn't just try to claw out my heart with her last comment. "Speaking of blasts from the past, your old agent, Paul Long, called me the other day, asking if you've snapped out of it yet. I told him I'd try to talk some sense into you now that it's all over."

Another jab to my soul. Over? As in being over the loss of the best woman ever? My pain will never be over. My fists clench. Feeling me tense, no doubt, Jax runs a comforting hand up and down my arm, and I visibly relax with a prolonged exhale. Morgan follows the gesture but keeps the conversation trained on me. "If you sign back with Paul and his agency, you wouldn't have to go through the whole draft hoopla in the spring. You'd have a contract the next day and be playing in the NHL already, like you should have been doing after your freshman year."

What she really means is playing in the NHL with her on my arm, the hockey player's trophy girlfriend. Or would I be her trophy? It's what Morgan envisioned since we first met, but her visions and mine all turned to shit after I lost my mother. After I'd promised on her deathbed that I'd get an education first.

How about your promises to me? Morgan had whined only weeks after the funeral, never even bothering to understand my grief. My loss. My own dreams dying along with my mom. How much it changed me … and in some ways for the better.

"No, I should have been with someone like Jax three years ago," I say calmly, clenching Jax's hand. I'm not even sure when I'd gripped it or if she'd taken my hand first, but it's the only thing tethering me against the onslaught of painful memories and introspection.

Morgan gives a short laugh. "Go ahead, settle for less, as usual. It's what you do best."

"That's what you've been doing," I tell her coolly, throwing a nod toward the football players and the Phi Pikes she reigns over. "I've upgraded." Not that Jax and I are really "together," but the difference between the two women couldn't be any clearer to me now.

Morgan gasps dramatically as if I physically hit her, and immediately, one of her sisters runs back to her side. While the woman nestled at my hip pipes in.

"Actually, Luke doesn't need you, me, or an agent," Jax says, taking a determined step toward Morgan, but I tug on our connected hands to keep her from springing on her like a cat. Although, wouldn't that be kind of awesome? But likely not as rewarding as Jax's verbal defense is. "Whether he's in scrubs or a jersey, maybe both, I've never met anyone so determined, loyal, and—"

"Spare me." Morgan cuts her off, raising a flat palm in the air so that it resembles a wall. "You can have him. He's no use to any woman during hockey season anyway."

Her comment has my eyes narrowing menacingly while Morgan and her friend giggle conspiratorially. Jax sends me a quizzical look, but I shake my head as if to suggest that I'll explain later. Eventually.

"By the way," Morgan adds with an evil smile, "I slept with Paul."

"I don't care who the hell you sleep with," I tell her, and it's the truth, but nevertheless, gross! Paul is in his forties and is a total man whore with a woman waiting in every city he represents. I guess now he has another in our little town here in Maine too. Back when he was courting me, he'd once sent a few of his girls up to my hotel room, but being stupidly smitten with Morgan at the time, I'd sent them packing. "Maybe Paul can introduce you to another hockey player because we have been and are over."

"Yeah, with a real professional hockey player." Morgan pivots to leave, but she can't keep it at just one letdown though. "Get your drunk slut out of here," she shoots back from over her shoulder.

When I move to take a step forward, both Jax and Tanner are holding me back. I hadn't even noticed Tanner's return. "Don't you fucking speak to her like that again," I roar, and Morgan's eyes go wide in alarm. I've never yelled at her or any woman, but it's enough. "Whether I was in the NHL or not, we would have broken up by now anyway because you can't love anyone but yourself."

In a flash of pink movement, Morgan grabs someone's drink and dramatically slings its liquid contents at me as if we're in a movie or something. It's beer, and fortunately, there wasn't much in it.

"Let's go!" Jax says, shoving at my chest in the direction of the door.

"Yes, you should go, *Jack*," Morgan adds sounding unfazed once more, her composed mask back in place, "and don't bother ever coming back here. You're now number one on our do-not-let-in list."

"Aww, I'm number one!" Jax exclaims cheerfully,

clapping her hands with mock excitement. "Thanks for caring and saving me from an STD, sis."

Tanner barks out a laugh at Jax's clapback but then covers his reaction by taking a gulp from his drink, the one he'd probably been bringing to me. I could have used it.

Grabbing my hand, Jax turns us away from Morgan and her crew, and we leave the party together, all eyes on our withdrawing backs.

LUKE

THE BITING wind that blasts us the moment we step outside does nothing to cool my blood from boiling over. I gulp in several cold breaths, trying to regain my control as we walk away from Greek Row. The thumping bass from the party slowly fades behind us.

Striding alongside me, Jax is punching and jabbing at the air. "Ugh! I could just pussy-punt her," she says, kicking at nothing.

I howl with laughter, my anger ebbing away like … like it was pussy-punted! OMG, I'm laughing harder than I have in years. I've never heard that expression before, but now I want it sewn onto a sweater.

Gathering her feisty, swinging hands, I bring Jax to a stop in the dimly lit quad. Her eyes glimmer beneath the glow of the lamp that barely lights the deserted area. "You were brilliant," I tell her, wishing I could better explain how truly remarkable I think she is, and not just due to her comebacks tonight sparring with Morgan. Although, I've never seen anyone stand up to the high queen like that.

Despite the heat of our touch, Jax's hands are freezing,

and it's only then that I realize she doesn't have a coat to put on over the sexy dress she's wearing. The one that almost brought me to my knees when I spotted her from across the room. I'd zeroed in on her like a bull to a waving red flag. The bold color bringing out the reddish strands in her auburn hair like magic. Magic? Yikes, listen to me.

I'd left my varsity jacket at home when I changed after the calendar shoot, so I can't offer my coat to wear either. Cupping her hands, I try rubbing heat into them. "Your hands are like ice."

She stops and gives a little gasp when I bring her hands to my mouth and blow, warming them with my breath. I pause for a second, the action feeling more intimate than when we'd kissed. I'm watching her over our joined grip, and something inside her melts. I can feel it. Or maybe it's me who's melting?

Jax starts to shiver, so I add my body heat as well and wrap my arms around her. It might be in the forties, but I'm not the least bit cold. Not with her in my arms.

"Th-thank you," she says, teeth chattering.

"No, thank you."

She looks up at me and our eyes lock and hold, drawing me in. "We know how to put on a show, that's for sure," she says with a slight chuckle. "Anytime you want me to pretend to be your girlfriend, you got it."

Pretend? Show? Hmm. I don't like that, and I step back, breaking our embrace. I don't acknowledge it though. I only nod. "I'm sorry about Morgan, I didn't mean to unleash her on you or to get you barred from her parties either."

"Oh, believe me, I won't miss them, and as for Morgan, she always acts ugly to any non Theta."

This is not surprising, and relief squelches my guilt. "Still, I'm sorry—"

"No," she insists, reaching up to capture my face between her cold, little hands. "I'm sorry about your mom."

I nod, accepting the meaningless condolence that I've heard hundreds of times since my mom died. The kindness and understanding in Jax's sincere stare tells me she means it, but like everyone else, she doesn't know what else to say. Not that there is anything anyone can say to ease the loss.

"How?" she asks, and I can almost drown in the warm, brown pools of her eyes that seem to be pulling me in, telling me that I can let go.

"Cancer. Just before the end of my freshman year."

"I had no idea," she says, letting her hands fall from my face to grasp my hands again. Before I can respond, Jax plunges ahead. "If I knew, I wouldn't have pushed you about the promise you made to her. I just thought it was something we all tell our parents … yes, I'll graduate first, no I won't drink, yada, yada. I didn't realize the beautiful, painful extent of it. And now I get why you'd choose healthcare as a career too. I can't—"

I capture her mouth in a fierce kiss, preventing her from continuing to wreak havoc on my aching heart with her understanding words. I have no idea when my heart even started getting tangled with hers. Probably when our tongues first did, or maybe when she twirled out on the ice with that sassy smirk of hers, or during the many times she told me that I'd see. I might not know when, but it is beating a fast tempo for her now.

The sensual connection between us is making my head spin. I start to pull away to try and explain myself, but she greedily bites at my bottom lip in retaliation for breaking our kiss, and I dive back in for more. More of her. My breathing is heavy as our lips press together again, and this time, it's like she has sucked the soul out of my body. I can taste our shared breath, feel the thud of our combined heartbeats, and the adrenaline pumping a raging fire through my veins. Until this point, I've only felt this alive out on the ice.

It's not until someone jeers "Get a room!" from somewhere out in the dark distance that our lips tear apart, but our bodies stay intertwined. I don't recall lifting her, but Jax's long legs are enveloped around my waist and my hands are scooping her fine ass, pressing her closer.

"They're probably right," I say reluctantly, my voice sounding grave. "Let me walk you back to your dorm."

Nodding, she uncrosses her ankles and slides down my front. I don't bother to hold in my groan. And the little brat has the nerve to giggle, which is why I have no qualms about swatting her butt to get her moving. Laughing, she takes a step, then stops abruptly.

"Oh, shoot! I forgot my roommate's boyfriend is visiting, and I said I'd find someplace else to crash for the night."

I almost swallow my tongue from the thoughts swarming my brain of Jax in my room, tucking her into my bed, her body naked under my jersey, but before I can dare suggest it, Jax is naturally talking.

"Oh! You know what? Go ahead and bring me to Cal Chase's room," she says, pointing her arm in the direction of Tasker Hall where my friend resides.

I literally stumble over my wooden feet. "Why the hell would I do that?"

"Normally, I'd crash at April's since she's the only one of us without a roommate, but her door is broken or something. So, she's been going through Cal's door since they have connecting singles. Now it's like one big room with the door finally open between them."

I'm not sure I fully understand her convoluted

explanation, but I fixate on her last comment about 'one big room' and a ménage à trois image is conjured, searing my brain. "Yeah, no."

"Yeah?" she repeats happily.

"No," I state flatly, not elaborating on why it's more like a fuck no. Because there is no way I'd be delivering her to my buddy late at night looking like a gift-wrapped present, and especially not after they've both had a few drinks.

"Oh," Jax says, looking confused, and that's when I notice her pupils are dilated and her eyes are slightly red, confirming my suspicions that she might have had more than a few. "How about the stinky couch in your common room?"

I snort. "Sure, let me leave you passed-out drunk with twenty jocks under one roof." Including her whatever he was, Diego.

"Hey!" Hands on her hips, Jax pushes back. "Despite what your crazy ex implied earlier, I'm not drunk."

"Tipsy, then," I amend.

She appears to mull the definition over for a second, then tilts her head in agreement. "Fine, now what?"

"You're sleeping with me."

Jax shrugs and drops her arms to her sides. "Okay."

"Okay, she says." Exasperated, I shove the hair away from my face. "How have you survived college? I meant you can sleep in my room."

Jax rolls her eyes and lets out a breathy laugh, then loops an arm through mine, leading me in the opposite direction of Tasker Hall and away from Cal Chase. A few minutes later, I ease open the front door of the Sports House, allowing her to enter my place for the third time. Another one of my rules broken, I'm now wondering how many more I'll break for Jax.

Upstairs, she surveys my bedroom with unconcealed interest. And while the ceiling slopes in places and I need to duck my head to look out the window, it's the largest room in the house and one of the perks of being president. Not only is it the biggest, but it also has a private bathroom and shower, which is especially useful when you've snuck a guest in. But I haven't tested the theory out … till tonight.

With good reason. The familiar, sweet scent of jasmine perfume fills my room and ignites a burn of desire in my body, a problem Jax seems to be totally unaware of as she snoops about without giving me a second glance.

"Neat as expected," Jax says with a hint of censure when she stops her circling.

Grr. What … am I supposed to have stuff lying on the floor just to prove I'm fun or something? "And I'm sure your room probably looks like a tornado hit it."

She nods, totally unaffected by my bite. "Yup, a hot mess like me."

"I didn't say that," I clarify.

"You were thinking it." Jax gives a short laugh, and then her gaze falls to my queen-size bed.

It's roomy, but not if we're both going to be in it. I suppose the gentlemanly thing to do would be to give her the bed and sleep on the floor, but I guess I'm no gentleman. "You can sleep under the covers, and I can sleep on top," I suggest instead.

Her lips turn up into a playful smirk. "But I like being on top."

Christ! It's not easy maintaining my usual icy glare of indifference when she's saying hot shit like that. I narrow my eyes at her. Hers, meanwhile, still have that vague, glassy look to them, but I can see the teasing laughter shining in them too. When I don't respond to her taunting, Jax shrugs and heads to the adjustable weight bench I use during my study breaks. With my crazy schedule, I cram in workouts whenever I can.

"Care to spot me," she dares, straddling the seat.

I gulp audibly at the mouthwatering sight of her thighs spread the width of the cushioned bench, her red dress hiking up to accommodate the wide stance. My gaze trails up her body, memorizing each detail, or perhaps I'm planning an attack? I'm not sure since it's hard to keep a single thought in my head, except the need to press into *her* right there on my bench press. My lustful thoughts clear some when I catch sight of the 150-pound weights balanced behind her. "A spot is all that would be left of you if you try and lift that."

Her nostrils flare at the challenge, but she backs down after reading the amount written on the weightlift plates too. Slumping her shoulders, she sits down on the seat with a humph. And now, thanks to her comment, I'm picturing us both sitting there, her hands gripping the metal bar while I lift her up and down with the thrust of my hips as she rides me.

Damn! This woman is going to be the death of me, but I guess there are worse ways to expire. "I'm going to take a quick shower and get the beer Morgan threw off me."

Pulling the sticky shirt up over my head, I toss it into the mini-size hockey net that I use as a laundry basket. Although I'd removed my shirt without thinking twice about it, I'm now relishing the way Jax is tracking my movements and sucking on her bottom lip. After the teasing view she just gave me, it's good to have switched sides.

"There are plenty of T-shirts in the cabinet, and I have waters and sports drinks in the mini fridge, so help yourself," I offer as I grab a clean towel.

She nods, not bothering to look toward the fridge or

chest of drawers, her stare solely focused on my naked chest. Good, I hope she suffers like I'm about to in a shower that I'll be setting to ice cold. I smirk and do an exaggerated flex of my arm, pointing it toward the direction of the bathroom. "I'll be in there if you need me."

I eventually hear her yell back, "I won't!" from the other side of the now-closed door. In the reflection of the bathroom mirror, I catch the smile plastered to my face and I almost don't recognize myself. It's been a while since I looked this carefree. Too long.

Once I wash up and pat myself dry, I wrap the towel low around my hips and grin, eager to tease Jax again. But when I open the door, I come to an immediate standstill. It appears I'm not the only one looking to tease.

Jax is wearing my old, Tier 1 jersey and nothing else. The hem stops at her thick and beautiful thighs, and I almost fall to my knees at the sight. The V-neck collar hangs low, revealing creamy skin and a bared shoulder. But the way it outlines her breasts, fuck me! Was she reading my mind earlier when I'd pictured almost the same sight? Reality is better. Much better. I swallow, trying to calm my breathing.

"Can I borrow a towel?" she asks with a husky laugh.

Forget my rules! I'm getting tired of fighting this attraction. I whip the towel off before she can say another word. I was pitching a tent anyway.

Jax gasps, and I cross the room in three steps. Her hands are already reaching for me, but mine are faster and I haul her up against my naked body. The feel of her pressed alongside me is pure torture, even with the jersey between us.

With a tug, she's pulling me forward and we fall backward on the bed, both of us laughing. Quickly, I shift my weight so I'm not crushing her. Her glorious, auburn hair is whipped across her face, and I reach up to smooth it away, revealing that gut-churning smile of hers. When Jax's direct gaze meets mine, I see a fire lit in them that matches mine and my laugh fades.

"I thought you like to be on top?" I joke, but of course Jax would take this as a challenge. I knew she would, but her daring still catches me off guard. Before I can blink, she slides out from under me and is straddling my hips. I hiss from the contact and the beckoning heat emanating through her panties. And when she moans my name, I involuntarily release pre-cum exactly where my dick is clamoring to break through the thin fabric.

Sitting up to meet her only causes Jax to sink more into my lap, deepening our contact and forcing the jersey to ride farther up her body, revealing the sexy curves of her ass. Unable to resist tasting her for another second, I grab the back of her head and tug her face forward for an urgent kiss. It turns feverish and wild immediately. Her arms band around my neck fiercely, tugging me closer, fingers curling into my hair. Seconds, minutes fly by, and we are a passionate tangle of limbs, breaths, and moans.

"Luke," Jax mutters against my lips, her nails digging into my back, and it feels like heaven.

Pulling my mouth away is the greatest test of my will ever. "Wait, wait, wait," I chant with a groan, already cursing myself for what I'm about to do. Lifting her easily by the hips, I place her alongside me. Her stunned expression is so cute that I'm leaning in to kiss her again, but no—gritting my teeth, I clench my fists to stop myself. "You've been drinking."

"So? Not that much and not for a while now anyway," Jax says, shooting me a look that clearly says she thinks I'm crazy. Maybe I am for stopping.

"I have a game tomorrow," I explain.

Jax nods and places little, wet kisses along my throat, and goose bumps form in her wake. "Not till tomorrow night." She purrs, her breath hot on my skin.

"I can't," I tell her between deep gasps for air. "I mean I *can*, but I can't."

"Huh?" She pulls back to look at me, her eyes still dazed, her hair and makeup mussed. It's how I imagine she'd look when she first wakes up, not that I've pictured that. Not often at least. With her shoulders drooped like they are now, she looks dwarfed next to me, and this observation only makes me want to roll back on top of her. But then I'd have to pull away again, and I doubt my willpower is that strong.

"I don't have sex during season," I blurt out.

Jax scrunches her nose like a bunny and considers me. "Winter?"

"Hockey."

"Oh, right," she says with a nod, then her eyes clear and go wide. "Ohhhh!"

I wonder if Morgan's snide comments earlier are now sinking in about me not being any use to a girlfriend during competitions. Stretching, I reach for a pillow to place over my lap. My own personal hockey stick hasn't gotten the memo that we're not playing today. The game has been canceled on account of the fact that I'm a masochistic idiot.

Taking a page out of Jax's book, I speak first before she can get her thoughts together. "Being pent up and sexually frustrated allows me to channel that energy and aggression out on the ice, for the team. My high school coach preached it, although I think he didn't want any of us knocking someone up and ruining our careers. But still, I've followed his advice since, and it's done well for me."

Jax nods again, but the wary look in her eyes tells me she's skeptical, so I try harder to make her understand. Shit, I hope she does! "Most athletes have rituals and superstitions, but really, it's about discipline."

Gathering my jersey nearer to her body, Jax stands, looking like a Grecian goddess ready to do battle. Her posture is haughty, but her bottom lip trembles slightly and the unexpected vulnerability is like a punch to my gut. "It's fine, Luke. If you didn't want to, you could have just said so and simply gone to sleep, or something."

Simply go to sleep? "Are you crazy?" I ask, releasing a shocked laugh, and I immediately know this was the wrong thing to say and do. "Wait!" I shout, rushing forward when Jax retreats to collect her dress draped across my workout bench. I manage to grasp her shoulders just before she can barricade herself inside my bathroom.

She freezes underneath my touch, turning rigid. "Look at me, Jacquie," I urge, gently spinning her around so she can see how serious I am. "I want to … I really, really want to. You're gorgeous and so fucking sexy." Releasing my grip, I gesture to the evidence of just how much I want to. And damn, when Jax lowers her lashes to look, I swell even bigger, proving my point. I fight back the urge to forget my stupid rule and just enjoy myself in her. The effort to contain myself leaves me weak.

"You're telling me … not having sex helps?" she asks, her expression softer, almost taking on a look of wonder.

"Yeah, it keeps both my heads in the game, so to speak. Lot of the greats do it, or don't do it, I should say. Muhammad Ali used to hold out for six weeks before a fight, and during last year's World Cup, coaches of several teams instituted teamwide bans." Of course, when I'd mentioned that news headline to Diego, he laughed for days. "Even Tom Brady has a strict twenty-four-hour no sex policy, which can go up to seventy-two hours for games of higher importance, and just look at his legendary career."

Jax tilts her head, scrutinizing my face for lies. Her expression is softer, at least, and the tension in my shoulders eases. I know her mind is racing, as usual, but at least she believes me, I can tell. She's no longer freezing me out. Instead, the open and confident Jax that I've come to expect has returned. "So, like nothing? Not even more of what we were doing before?"

"Not without getting blue balls," I admit, shoving a hand through my tangled hair. Jax huffs out a short laugh, evidently enjoying the idea of my discomfort, but that's of my own doing, or partially, at least. The sexy cock tease in front of me is half to blame. Bending down, I pick up my discarded towel and drape it over my hips again. But now that my lust is somewhat under control, a sense of loss and dread fills me. "Yeah, not really conducive to a normal relationship, hmm?"

Astonishingly, she shakes her head. "What's normal?"

"Typical then," I correct.

"Maybe, maybe not," Jax says with a shrug, her eyes sharp on mine. "But now at least it finally makes sense."

"What does?"

"Why a hunk like you isn't up to his neck in tits and ass every night."

I burst out laughing. Who says this stuff? "God, woman. You never fail to surprise me."

"Good." Leaning up on her toes, she stops my laughter with a quick peck on the lips. "Now, my turn for a cold shower, and then we can get some sleep. You have a big game tomorrow."

With a classic Jax smile, she snatches the towel from my waist and heads into the bathroom with it, leaving me gawking. Sighing, I pull on a pair of gym shorts and adjust myself to some lesser degree of discomfort. Then I go in search of the school throw that I got at an alumni relations fundraiser last year. I'd rather use Jax as a blanket tonight, but it will have to do.

Jax emerges later, looking fresh-faced and carefree. She's wearing my jersey again too. Except that it's not draped open like it was before, and I silently mourn the previous view. Yup, I really am a masochist. But her wearing my clothes, smelling like my soap, makes it feel like she belongs here, with me.

"Good night," she says sweetly, then slips under the covers like she's at a sleepover party with her bestie or something. Son-of-a-Stanley Cup!

I manage a grunt back. Even with the covers separating us and the few inches of space, I don't know how I'm ever going to sleep with her next to me. Just great. I'm going to be exhausted tomorrow, but not for any of the fun reasons I'd put a stop to.

Meanwhile, the source of my dirty thoughts isn't having trouble sleeping. She's snoring slightly within minutes, her breath shallow and steady.

Longest. Night. Ever.

15

JAX

OF ALL MY wacky Jacquie ideas, this has to be the stupidest. One of those scenarios you imagine will be sexy, but in reality … ugh, I should just go.

Perched atop an ancient, wooden massage table in a semi-lit storage room, I adjust the hem of the team jacket I'm wearing and clutch the cell phone in my lap. My thumb hovers over the green send icon to my drafted text message. Still unsent, I reread it for the hundredth time.

As far as seductions go, this is the D-list version, no matter how much I've rehearsed it in my head. The room smells like mold, and I've counted the broken hockey sticks lined up against the wall twice now. But I really want to show Luke that I support his sports celibacy, and I stupidly thought this would be the perfect way to help fuel him tonight. But I'm learning reality vs fantasy is not the same thing.

I was tempted to ask Emerson if there was any scientific evidence to support Luke's no-sex superstition, but I ran into April first and confided in her instead. She hadn't been as shocked as I was to learn about Luke's post-party confession though. Instead, she mentioned something about how Hemingway believed sex sapped his creativity too. So, maybe Luke is onto something here, and if he wants to be sexually frustrated, then I figured maybe I could help up the ante for him. And despite my protests to my friends … well, I think there is more than just a little something between me and Luke. But since when have I ever cared about labels? At least not until I met Luke, and now, I want to be claimed all over by him.

For fuck's sake, just do it! Fine. I stab the send button before I can chicken out. Maybe Luke won't even see my message before his game, and I can go wait in the stands like a normal woman would do.

> Me: Meet me in the storage closet across from Tavish's offices.

> Luke: Who dis? New phone.

At another time and place, I'd probably have found his teasing funny, but I'm so jittery that I'm in no mood to laugh. Our previous conversation about distributing the calendar is clearly in the chat history above, so he knows very well who this is.

> Shut up and hurry!

> My game is in 20.

> Then get moving, Captain.

The seconds tick by slower than the last few minutes of class, and I start to doubt if he's going to show. Maybe it's for the best.

When the knob turns and the door eases open, I scramble to strike a sexy pose and push past my nervousness. Holy crap! He looks good in his uniform, even if his gorgeous, blue eyes are looking at me like I'm crazy. Perhaps I am, for him.

Without a sound, Luke glances over his shoulder, then steps inside the small room, closing the door behind him with a faint click.

"Hello?" he whispers, hesitant.

"You … um … you said being sexually frustrated increases your game," I state, not making it a question, but Luke nods anyway, his intense gaze holding mine. "And tonight is an important match."

He nods a second time, and my heart rate kicks up another notch. His eyes watching my movements, I unzip the bulky Thunderblades' hockey jacket I'm wearing to reveal that there is nothing on underneath. I hold my breath, waiting for a response, but despite my wild imaginings, I didn't expect his reaction.

Luke drags in a deep breath and falls to his knees in front of me. His fisted hands knock the wooden surface on both sides of my opened knees. He's clenching them so hard, I can see his knuckles going white.

Not gonna lie. After years of being ignored as a teenager, to have a man of Luke's strength, discipline, and size kneeling before me is hard to fathom and heady as fuck. His breathing is labored, and I watch him try to pull himself together, to compose his wild, hungry eyes, but I refuse to let him go back to his normally cool and controlled self.

With more daring than I give myself credit for, and a bit drunk on the power I have over him, I spread my legs wider for his viewing, brushing his balled fists aside in the process. If his gaze was intense before, his sharp focus now has wetness pooling right where he is staring. Oh shit! If it continues, I might slide right off the edge of the table.

Not bothering to look up, he asks with the tiniest bit of tenderness and awe in his voice, "This is for me?" His breath teases my wet, sensitive skin and I moan my confirmation. At least I think I do because I can barely hear my response over the thudding in my ears.

"Can I have a taste?" His silky, deep voice slides its way down my spine, bringing my entire body to attention. I nod, unable to break his gaze.

"You may," I grant, sounding haughtier than I intended. It feels like we're playing a game of Mother May I, the dirty version. I almost laugh at the thought, but it turns into a startled eek when Luke grips my thighs, massaging them, his fingers getting closer to my opening. Mesmerized, he leans in and licks my clit. I gasp all over again, sensations twisting and turning inside me. Only when he tosses both of my legs over his shoulders do I realize he plans to do more than just taste.

"Luke! Your game!" But he only grunts in confirmation, not the least bit concerned. "Don't you dare start something you can't finish," I warn, and when I look down, he's grinning up at me from between my legs, and the sensual sight leaves me sucking in air.

Chuckling, Luke parts my slit open with his hot tongue, and I almost fall flat back onto the table. "Don't worry, sweet tea, I won't leave you frustrated like me. No reason why you can't be satisfied while I feed my hunger too."

"But … but you only have like ten minutes left," I remind him in an almost desperate-sounding plea.

He jerks my butt to the edge of the table and rasps into my opening, "Challenge accepted!"

"That wasn't a ch—"

"Shh!" He hums into my clit, the vibrations singing through me. "You'll have to be quiet. Unless you want the guys out there to hear."

The thought kicks my imagination up a gear, and I'd be lying if my pussy didn't pulse at the thought, but I shake my head and bite my bottom lip, trying to keep my moans in. "I'll be quiet."

"Good girl, because I want to be the only one to hear you cum."

My arms clench his muscular waist and I nearly moan louder at his the good girl.

Hot damn, he won't need ten minutes, or even five, talking dirty like that, especially not with his palms roaming up and down my sides, then grazing up to my breasts. Like he has all the time in the world, he leisurely swipes back and forth over my nipples. I relax—no, melt—beneath his touch, and then he is licking me in what I can only call a merciless devouring, creating an overload of sensations that no vibrator has ever achieved.

The flicking of his thumb on my clit, and his tongue sliding left and right, vacuuming my skin in between his greedy lips, is already sending me close to the edge. I've never had a man who could turn me on like this, who could make me feel so much with only his hands and his tongue. His big, calloused fingers press inside me, stretching me. I can hear the rasps of my heavy breathing, but I have no will to tamper down my reactions, the sensations. I can only feel, and I feel like I'm on fire. And the only way to put out a fire …

I go from panting to almost not breathing. Stilling, I concentrate on my building orgasm and bite my lip painfully to keep from crying out. Despite my efforts, a moan threatens to tear out of my throat. Possibly sensing it, Luke replaces his tongue with the pad of his thumb and leans up to silence my scream with his mouth. I cum so hard on his hand, all while sucking his lips for air, our breaths and taste combining.

Luke pulls back and places sweet, light kisses on my lips and down my throat, and I fall farther. When I come back down into my body, I hear Luke laugh one of his deep, wonderful, rare laughs. "And with some time to spare too. Sorry I can't pull off a hat trick, but another time. That's a promise."

Rising up, he peels his white-and-red practice jersey up over his head like a Herculean god, revealing a tantalizing sight I could have used for extra ammunition a few moments ago. Well, not that I needed it, but still, the sight reignites my desire. Balling up the jersey, Luke uses the material to soothingly wipe between my legs. After which, he boldly brings the fabric up to his nose and inhales it in deeply. I'm not one to blush, but I feel my face heating. I refuse to be embarrassed, though, as I've never seen or experienced anything hotter than this … than him. I guess fantasy and reality might be the same after all. But even I hadn't imagined this outcome.

"You're unusually quiet," Luke says with a grin. Reaching forward, he chucks me affectionately under the chin, then gathers my jacket together, zipping it all the way up. "There," he mumbles with a satisfied nod, "our little secret."

He smirks at me and my tongue-tied self, then turns to leave. He stops once he places a hand on the door handle. Turning around, he fixes me with a determined stare. I've never seen his clear, blue eyes appear so dark. "Every goal, every steal, every bodycheck will be because of you, for you."

Before I can come up with an intelligent response, or a sound, for that matter, Luke eases the door open just enough to squeeze out. I'm thankful because, for once, I have no freakin' words. None. My brain is mush, just like my bones currently.

I glance about the dark room. Everything is the same from when I first closed myself in here. But also … nothing is the same. Puck me!

16

LUKE

THANKS TO JAX'S surprise striptease and my resulting feast, I've morphed into a savage beast. Releasing the restless animal that prowls inside me, I'm tearing up the ice and plowing through any player who dares to get in my way. I've already been penalized for charging, boarding, and cross-checking, but I've also scored twice with no assists, so Coach Tavish has stayed out of it.

It takes two of my teammates to pull me off Hoover University's lead defenseman. When I'm sent to the sin bin for roughing, I'm thankful for the chance to control myself. It's not easy, though, when I can still smell her on me.

Not only on my lips, but because I'm wearing the practice jersey from earlier underneath my uniform. Smirking, I snag the fabric out from under my collar, lock eyes with Jax in the stands, and give it an exaggerated whiff. Fuck it smells good.

From the way her eyes have gone wide, I know I've shocked her. Good. She needs to know that while I might be temporarily celibate, I'm still a red-blooded man with needs. And fuck, do I need her. Every time I think about

Jax wearing my jersey pulled tight over her tits, I get rock hard. And now that I know what she looks like underneath? Hissing out a jagged breath, I grind my teeth in a useless effort to tamp down the lust and adrenaline raging through me.

With my schedule and workload, I'd stupidly thought I couldn't possibly handle any other distractions in my life, but I was wrong. Jax is a good kind of distraction, the sort that makes the hard shit easier to swallow. Thanks to Morgan, I'd assumed women were nothing but stress and mind games, but everything is so easy with Jax. And even though she occupies most of my thoughts, I'm still working hard, I'm still playing. Tonight's scoreboard is proof she's not messing with my game but helping it. Chuckling, I glance up at our lead.

I guess you could say Jax is sort of like dessert—there always seems to be room no matter how full you thought you were. And damn, I'm starving. No more fighting it. Jax and I might have been unexpectedly thrown together, and are opposites in so many ways, but there is no denying our connection. Even if I'm black and white and she's a rainbow unicorn, I don't care. Wise or not, I need to see it through.

Even before today's closet encounter, I'd already decided to invite Jax to join me in Vermont for Thanksgiving since she doesn't have plans for the holiday. Although, my reasons aren't altogether altruistic, especially not now. I was originally thinking she'd be a welcome buffer between my dad and I during the break and conference, but now … I'm hoping she can continue to fuel this beast within me during my Frost Fest games too. And well, I just like being around her, even with her litany of questions. Seriously, who would have thought, after only a few short weeks, the idea of a mere week apart would seem too long to go without seeing her? Even more surprising is that this revelation doesn't even scare me, although wondering if Miss Carefree Jax is up for more does.

I was planning on casually bringing the trip up before today's game, but her sexy stunt threw all thoughts straight out of my head and to my groin. My ego soars, recalling how I'd turned the tables on her surprise seduction, though, and I'm grinning in the sin bin like an unrepentant maniac.

Fifteen seconds left on the timer. I pound my fists against the glass in applause when Blake accomplishes a takeaway, despite the power play stacked against us.

"Oh, what an electrifying game!" the announcer booms over the speakers to the crowd, and I stand, waiting to spring from my cage. I haven't seen this many people in the stands since I started playing for the Thatcher Thunderblades, which is also thanks to Jax's efforts.

The second I'm released from the penalty box, I come out charging. Hoover's right winger wisely veers left and out of my way.

"Ladies and gentlemen, number 22, Luke Prescott, is back in."

I usually tune the announcer out, but today, it feels like he's spurring me into action.

"This is ice hockey at its finest! Hoover sets up in the defensive zone in preparation for the Thunderblades' play that's about to come."

Tanner delivers a short pass, and I'm back in control of the puck. Using quick and agile movements, I send a long shot to Cayden, then break away to wait on the other side of the net. "Accuracy, power, and timing," I chant silently, waiting for my opportunity.

"The puck is at the blue line, passed over to Luke. Luke winds up, the crowd's on their feet! He's aiming for that top corner, the

goaltender's ready. He shoots—oh, what a laser of a shot! The puck rockets past the diving goalie, and … SCORES!"

My teammates collide into me for a group hug, celebrating our inevitable win and better ranking at next week's competition.

"That's it, folks!" the announcer drags out, eliciting more cheers from the audience. It's thrilling and I'm laughing. I'm downright laughing on the ice. It's been ages since I felt this free.

When the horn blasts, announcing the end of the third period, I know I've won more than just the game, and I'm looking up at my prize. Jax is hopping and cheering in celebration, and while her camera is pointed toward the ice, her gaze is eating mine up in return.

17

JAX

"Buckle up," Luke says, sounding very much like a worried parent, but I keep this amusing thought to myself and click my seat belt into place as instructed.

It's hysterical. Luke looks serious even when driving despite the casual Thunderblades baseball cap he's wearing, which has his dark blond hair curling around his ears. Seeing his brow furrowed in concentration while backing out of the parking spot almost has me laughing out loud, but somehow, I contain myself. Actually, his methodical ways are becoming endearing. Earlier, I'd watched with my mouth open as he skillfully arranged our bags and his bulky equipment, leaving space to still see out the rear window.

Naturally, Luke's Toyota RAV4 is as clean and tidy as his bedroom. My beat-up car, on the other hand, has hangers and clothes piled in the back seat and empty coffee cups occupying every possible cup holder. Note to self: Clean it up before Luke sees it. No point in confirming what he already assumes. Maybe I'll even put those cute car freshener clips in the vents too. I smile to myself, imagining his shock at finding my vehicle looking spotless. Not that we have plans to be in my car, but I figure at some point, he'll see it since we're sort of dating. At least, I think we are.

I'm assuming this not only because he rocked my world in a storage closet, but we've been texting nonstop since— from dirty to flirty stuff and about everything and nothing. I glance over at Luke's profile and consider. Come to think of it, we've seen each other almost every day since my comms project started. And here I am, joining him and his family for Thanksgiving break at a rental home in Vermont near the tournament. Yup, I'm meeting the parents! Or parent, rather. Nothing says relationship more than that. Right?

Boy, do I hate living in the land of uncertainty. I tell myself to chill and see where things go naturally, but I'm not listening, which is nothing new. Although, my desire to define a relationship sure the heck is. Normally, I'm used to having the upper hand with guys, so this is uncharted territory for me.

"Soooo, what did you tell your dad about me joining?"

As soon as the question leaves my lips I tense up, worried about what he's going to say and putting myself on a ledge like this.

"I didn't," Luke says, not taking his eyes off the road.

"Wait, he knows I'm coming, right?"

"Yes, of course I told him that."

I slump my shoulders in relief. "But nothing else?" I ask, fishing for an actual response.

Luke simply shakes his head, and I have the sudden urge to hit him with the unopened notebook resting on my lap. Guys! I don't mean to stereotype a whole gender, but they are the worst at communicating.

I try again. "What's he going to think of me being there?"

"Whatever he wants to think," Luke says with an indifferent shrug, but his grip on the steering wheel tightens, and I have no idea what to make of it. If he's this annoyed by the topic, then why did he invite me to tag along when, surely, it's going to come up? "It's not like he sought my opinion when he started dating my aunt."

My ears perk up at the word dating, but hold on. What did he just say? "Whoa, what now?"

Luke merely nods again. Forget hitting him with my notebook. I want to shake the answers out of him. If he wasn't driving, I might have done it too. "Your dad is seeing your mom's sister?"

"No."

Great, and we're back to his usual one-word responses. "No," I echo at a loss. "Ew, is he dating *his* sister?"

"Gross, no!" Luke says, almost veering into the other lane. After collecting himself for a moment, he finally elaborates further. "She's not really my aunt, not by blood. She was my mother's best friend, and we've always called her Aunt Kathy. So, that's who she's always been to me."

"This must be quite the change then."

Luke snorts as if to suggest what I said is an understatement. My mom had a couple of boyfriends whom I called "uncles" as a little kid, but I don't think that's quite the same thing. It's also different for me since my parents divorced when I was two, so I never really knew them together. "But they didn't, I mean, not till after she passed, right?"

"Yeah," Luke agrees, but still not sounding pleased about it. "They got together last year after they started attending a weekly support group together. Then, I guess they decided to continue to support one another or something."

Last year would mean that his dad started dating two years after his wife died. That's not so bad, but I can understand Luke not being okay with it. Seeing his dad with someone else—anyone—must be difficult. We drive in silence for a little while, both processing this. I know it's not my place, but I can't help but feel sorry for his dad and what they've all gone through in the wake of her death.

"It's kind of nice, though, no? At least they both loved your mom and can comfort one another and keep each other company in her absence. Better than him dating some stranger whom you'd have to spend this weekend with too. You know, like a random woman who didn't know your amazing mother or you."

Luke purses his lips but remains silent. Once again, I tell myself that's enough intruding on my part. Back off, Jax. He is not a problem to fix. This time, I do listen.

Ten minutes later, just when I'd given up expecting a response, Luke speaks. "I hadn't thought about it that way. And this might sound cheesy, but lately, I've started wondering if it's my mom's doing. Like maybe she's matchmaking the two from up there or something."

"Maybe she is." Smiling at his theory, I reach over the middle console to place what I hope is a comforting hand on Luke's leg.

"Thanks," Luke says, turning his head briefly to glance at me before bringing his gaze back to the road.

The pain and tenderness I glimpsed in his eyes has my heart constricting. "For what?"

"For an outside perspective and for coming with me this weekend. We're not even there yet, and I'm already feeling better about it. I've been dreading this trip, but now

—" I squeeze his leg in understanding. "Aunt Kathy, I mean, Kathy, is going to love you, by the way."

"Really?" I ask, and even I can hear the excitement in my voice, the pesky need for approval as my hand caresses up and down his thigh.

Luke nods and then smirks. "She talks almost as much as you do. And the two of you together?" Luke grimaces. "My poor dad has no idea what's about to hit him."

I laugh, knowing Luke doesn't mean this disparagingly, and I'm relieved I won't be entering a hostile family scenario after all. "And thanks for saving me from cafeteria turkey and being alone in an empty dorm."

I can't seem to stop touching him. I started out wanting to comfort him, but the feel of him is addictive. Teasingly, I slide my palm to grip his muscular upper thigh. "I guess road head is out of the question?"

"Shit!" Luke swears, swerving again, and I burst out laughing. I was only half-teasing, though, because the idea, picturing it, has *me* excited. Even more so once I spot the bulge forming in Luke's pants.

"As soon as the season is over," Luke says, his voice husky, "I'll drive you wherever you want to go, sweetheart. That's a promise."

I'm not sure if it's the endearment, his hinting at future plans, or the idea of sucking him off, but my head is swimming, and I'm burning from the inside out. Nodding, I slip my hand away and fold it primly on my lap.

"I'd like that," I practically purr, licking my lips at the thought.

Staring straight ahead, Luke shifts in his seat and curses once more under his breath. "Believe me, I'd like it even more."

His admission has me preening in my seat. "Just give me a holler," I say, and immediately contemplate smacking my own forehead with my notebook for sounding like a dork.

Luke is smiling though. "Hey, I've been meaning to ask you. Where are you from?"

"All over. We moved around every couple of years. My mom was a military brat, so I guess it's in her bones."

"Ever lived down South?"

"Why?" I ask dubiously, but already guessing the reason. It's not the first time I've been asked this since living in the Northeast.

"Because every once in a while, I catch a Southern accent."

"Oh, bless your heart," I say, layering the twang on thick, and Luke chuckles. "Yeah, I'm originally from Valdosta, Georgia and spent some time in 'Or-lins' too."

"Hmm," Luke mumbles, his smile getting bigger.

"What?"

"Nothing."

"Come on," I urge, giving him a little elbow poke until he relents with a smile.

"No wonder you're pretty as a peach and as shocking as Mardis Gras."

Who knew you could laugh and blush at the same time, but that's what I'm doing. "Be careful. If you say poetic stuff like that, April is going to rope you into performing at the next open mic night with her."

Luke's expression sobers quicker than the blink of an eye. "Nope, those words are just for you."

And I'm melting again. Who is this charmer occupying Luke's seat? I clear my throat to cover the silence and my own awkwardness as I try to recall what we were talking about. "It's been years since I was down 'yonder' though. Last stop was Portland, Oregon, and now my main residence is Thatcher. The rest of my stuff is stuck in a storage unit out in California with my mother and new boyfriend. I'm going to go see them for Christmas break, but I'm really counting on this summer internship program so I can stay in New England before starting senior year."

Luke nods, his head briefly swiveling to glance at me again, and I'm surprised by the shy expression on his face. "After graduation, I'm hoping to sign with a team up here and am only applying to med schools in the area too."

"Cool," I say breezily, but considering the way my stomach flipped, you'd think he suggested we live together. When did I get like this? Awkward and pathetic. It's as if I was in love.

The thought hits me like a thunderbolt—a Thatcher Thunderbolt—and the single word "love" seems to be ricocheting around in my skull like a pinball.

Dating. Relationships. Love. My head is spinning.

18

LUKE

My hockey sense has saved me once again.

Or maybe it's something else at work here—lust, infatuation, love. Whatever the hell you want to call it, having Jax with us for the Frost Fest Conference has been a game changer.

The Thunderblades have already advanced to the final round of the playoffs, no thanks to Tanner Bouche who barely showed up during our game versus the MNU Pagans. He let an opportunity slip through his stick—an open pass he normally would make with ease, but he was too busy glancing up at the stands like a noob and letting their prick of an enforcer Hollingsworth rough him up. Tanner better get his head in the game, especially if he thinks he's going to be Captain next year when I'm gone. I make a mental note to talk to him privately before our final match tomorrow, but for now I push him and the team from my mind and focus being in the present.

It's been the nicest Thanksgiving break I've had since my mom passed and again I credit that to Jax being here to ease the tension between me and my pops.

The vacation rental Kathy found for us is a quaint, woodsy cabin surrounded by trees still adorned with the rich colors of fall. Not all of the oaks, but more than I was expecting for this time of year. When we arrived, my dad not so tactfully pointed out that the cabin has three bedrooms, but I shut him up when I asked which one Kathy was taking. Much to my delight and endless frustration, Jax and I have been bunking together. I never thought I liked to snuggle, but with Jax in my arms … well, it just hits differently.

The place has a game room, too, with an air hockey table, which Jax found amusing. She posted a video of me playing on it as a "warm-up" to the real tournament and our followers ate it up with likes and comments of encouragement. Although, for a second there, I almost got my ass handed to me by Jax, but I came through in the end. Hopefully, the same goes for my next real hockey game. Nope, no more shop talk for a bit.

The cabin's fully-equipped kitchen made today's delicious turkey meal possible, and even though I'm in the living room area with my dad watching football after dinner, I can hear Jax and Kathy chatting as they cut into the store-bought pumpkin pie we're having for dessert. It looked so good that I've already requested two slices. We offered to help, but they shooed us out of there with directions to add more logs to the fire.

"She's not at all like Morgan," my dad states a little too loudly over the crackling fireplace. "You said Jacquie was here because of an internship, but looks like there is more to it and to *her* than riding your coattails."

Was that what Morgan was doing? Maybe. "She's nothing like Morgan," I reiterate, but my mind returns to the other part of his statement. "I didn't realize that's what you thought of Morgan."

"Wasn't my place, but now that she's out of the picture, I can't say I miss her," he says with a sheepish smile.

We don't usually talk about personal stuff like this. That was more my mother's department, but I've noticed him trying harder in her absence. I feel bad we aren't closer, but his hectic schedule and my mom's illness kept him busy. I suppose my countless travel games didn't help either.

My dad makes a nervous glance toward the kitchen door, then back to me. "I wanted to thank you for being nicer to Kathy."

"Thank you for not calling her Aunt Kathy," I say with a chuckle, and then we both grimace.

"I know it must have been awkward at first—it was for us too—but it means a lot that you're being more supportive now."

"That was Jax's doing, but I was starting to get used to the idea," I admit.

He nods, and we both turn back to the TV and let the silence stretch out for a few plays.

"Luke, uh, the support group I go to urges us not leave things unsaid with those who are still here with us, and since it's just the two of us, now is as good a time as any," my dad says, turning in his recliner to look at me.

I was told so often how much I looked like my mother, I forgot that his eyes are almost identical to mine in color and shape. Currently, they are pinning me with an intense stare that I also tend to do sometimes. Interesting.

"I wanted to tell you how proud I am of you," my dad says after clearing his throat. "You know hockey was never my thing, and that I didn't participate in sports when I was younger, but proud is how I've always felt seeing you play. Your mother was too."

"Thank you," I say, choking up slightly. I knew she was,

but him? "I never asked you to love hockey though." Just me.

"I know. You never asked for anything. You're a good boy, and I'm sorry I didn't say it more often. But most of all, I'm sorry we let our fears become yours."

"What do you mean?"

"The whole backup plan speeches and ultimatums. It's just that your mom and I struggled so much financially after she was first diagnosed with cancer, we didn't want you having to go through the same one day. Or having to work and leave your own family like I did in order to make ends meet. You want better for your kids, you know? We were so relieved when you earned this scholarship, but for us, hockey was a means to an end. I don't think either of us understood you weren't done with hockey … that you still wanted more than a degree."

I nod, unable to believe this is my clam of a dad opening up. Hockey had carried me through the worst of my grief when I'd lost my mother, and completing my degree gave me direction when I was lost, purpose. But perhaps I don't need that anymore. Ever since Jax's pestering and belief in me, I've started to question what I really want. Following his lead, I try to voice what I'm coming to realize too. "College was just the next step for me in terms of playing hockey, not my last. A steppingstone."

"I know. I realize that now," my dad says, still fixing me with an intense, icy-blue stare. "Don't get me wrong, I'm glad you're earning your degree—magna cum laude even —but if you didn't … it's your life, son, not ours. Your mom could never have imagined all the offers that you received at the end of your first year. My head was spinning over them, and I bet even she would have had a change of heart too. You'd found your own safety net without us."

I know he can't speak for her, but the familiar tightness around my heart relents. Simply hearing him say this feels like an absolution of sorts to the promise I made, the pressure I've felt.

"You have my approval for whatever you decide to do, Luke, but I guess you're in the home stretch now anyway," he says, smiling and bobbing his head.

"The closing minutes," I correct, phrasing the expression into hockey terminology. "Or you could say the final period."

"The final period," he repeats, mulling it over.

"Thank you," I say, for lack of anything better to convey my feelings. It's a lame response, but my dad nods and returns his attention back to the game as if he hadn't just thrown darts at my heart.

In perfect timing, Jax takes this lull in our conversation to reappear with plates of pumpkin pie. Attuned as she is, she halts, glancing between us. "Are we interrupting anything?" she asks. "We can put these back in the fridge."

"No, no," my dad coos, reaching out for his plate when Kathy enters, holding two slices as well. "Now that you're here Jax, I've been meaning to ask you two something important."

"Dad!" I groan, fearing his support group might have opened him up a little too much. I also don't want him asking questions about us quite yet. At least not until Jax and I had those discussions ourselves.

"It has to be said," my dad snaps forcefully, and I blink back in surprise. Shooting a glance over at Jax, I watch her stiffen, bracing herself for an inquiry.

Dragging the moment out, my dad clears his throat, and that's when I notice his eyes are sparkling with amusement. "What is this about Diesel's son attending Thatcher?"

His question has Jax releasing a bubble of nervous laughter.

"You know that's my favorite band," he continues undeterred.

"Well, Mr. Prescott, not only does Steely Nash go to our college, but he's also dating my best friend, and I managed to get him to agree to sing the anthem at Luke's last home game of the year," Jax boasts with a proud smirk.

"Bravo!" my dad says, clapping. "You'll have to send me a link to the video after."

"Or maybe we'll drive up for it!" Kathy exclaims and my dad nods.

Shocked and yes, a little excited too now, I chime in. "Coach is so happy about all the buzz Jax has created for the Thunderblades, you'd think we'd won the Stanley Cup."

"I can imagine," my dad says approvingly. "Sounds like you're a shoo-in for that internship contest then, huh?"

"I hope so," Jax says, crossing her fingers on both hands. "I really want to stay over on this coast for the summer and build up my resume before I graduate."

I want her to stay nearby as well, and mentally, I cross my fingers too.

19

JAX

You know how there are those times in your life when you can sort of feel fate watching you? When all your hard work and planning has amounted to a particular moment, but now, all you can do is wait and hope that it turns out okay? Well, today is one of those pivotal times for me, and I suppose for Luke too.

It's the Thunderblades' last home game before winter break, and several scouts are here to witness him play, along with most of the student body. It's a sold-out event, and Professor Clark is in the packed stands this evening too. From my seat on the team bench, my gaze flicks over to Clark's reserved seat, which I selected for her since it has a perfect view of the ice and the jumbotron video screen. I'm relieved to see she's smiling and speaking with the people next to her. All promising signs.

Speaking of signs, literal ones, I glance up at the championship banner from Frost Fest hanging high above the rink, and my heart fills with pride. Luke wanted that winning banner flying before wrapping up his final season, and he did it. Amazing! Now, hopefully it's my turn to achieve a goal. Figuratively, not literally. I'll go ahead and leave the actual goal scoring to the Thunderblades.

Holding up Emerson's clipboard she lent me, I review my list of to-dos and am comforted to note that everything is running according to schedule. Most of the fundraising calendars were distributed in time for the new year, and the few that remain are being sold up front by Emerson and April. I enlisted their help amid promises that I'd owe them in return. I fear April is ready to claim my firstborn, but Em, on the other hand, said having Steel perform tonight was thanks enough. So, I prearranged for her to leave the table and head backstage to watch Steel sing in about—I check my watch—thirty seconds.

Confidently, Steel emerges from the Zamboni entrance as the announcer introduces him as tonight's singer of the national anthem. We placed a mat over the ice for him to stand on, and he takes his mark along with his electric guitar. He plans to do the anthem like Jimi Hendrix did at Woodstock. At least that's how Steel explained it when he sent me a YouTube clip of the epic performance. I got to listen earlier to Steel's rock rendition during the soundcheck, and I'm confident his riffs will get the crowd hyped up for the action to come. Yup, he's only on his first pause, and the chorus of whistles and whoops when he hits the whammy bar confirms it. The reactions to the live stream are blowing up my phone's notifications as well.

Yes, everything seems to be clicking into place as the Thatcher Thunderblades take the ice to thunderous applause. For the next bit, all I can do is watch and record. Now, with only minutes left in the first period, the game is tied, and Luke has remained out of the penalty box for a change. He's still playing like an uncaged beast, but at least he's not aggressively fouling the other team like he did during the conference playoffs. Then again, I took it easy on him today, and if my ego is overinflating with sexual power, well then, guilty as charged. Go ahead, lock me up, preferably in another storage closet with Luke.

I literally shake my head to clear my lusty thoughts and bring my attention back to the run of show listed on my clipboard. The theater crew and I decided to do the great duck drop after instead of between periods. This way, it will keep everyone staying till the very end and should be easier to clean up without worrying about the game restarting. I'm not the least bit sorry that I went ahead and removed the grand prize kiss, too, because while Luke and I still haven't had "the talk," I'll be damned if anyone else is going to be kissing my man. And the thought of me kissing anyone else is as appealing to me as one of April's poetry readings and Em's science fairs. Sorry, girls.

Speaking of kissing … I confirm the time left on the clock and search for Asif and his AV group. The audience Kiss Cam bit should be starting during the first break. I nod when I find Asif standing by the camera rig and radio him on the walkie-talkie to make sure he's set.

"Yes, boss, over and out," Asif confirms, sounding like a truck driver as he speaks into the remote.

"Roger," I mimic in return, then clip my set back on the waistband of my jeans and make room as Luke and his teammates begin to return to the players' bench just as the Kiss Cam zeroes in on the first couple in the audience. People are pointing up at the screen and clapping with each featured smooch. Yes! They are engaged, and I couldn't be happier.

I'm laughing and cheering along with the crowd when an elderly man shocks his wife with a passionate kiss. A moment later, though, I'm caught doing a double take when Asif and his camerawoman pop into my line of vision and pan to Luke, who is suddenly next to me and not back in the locker room as expected.

Luke's full lips twitch into a smile, and laughter dances in his eyes. "Come on, show me what you got," he says over the applause, mimicking what I told him during the calendar photo shoot.

"All right, Ice Man, take this!" Leaning up on my toes, I grab a fistful of his jersey and pull him down to meet me. Our lips fit together like missing puzzle pieces. His hands are on my hips, pulling me in tighter. Vaguely, I register the crowd's cheers in the distance growing and then fading, but I can't bring myself to stop kissing him.

Eventually, one of us pulls away, although I'm too frazzled to confirm who. Luke is grinning down at me, and it takes a moment for me to realize Asif and the camera guy are no longer here.

"You did this?" I sputter, and Luke nods with a wide grin that causes my heart to flutter. "But ... but you don't like attention!"

Leaning down so that our eyes are level, Luke brushes back my hair and shrugs his padded shoulders. "I wanted to surprise you," he says. Then, almost as an afterthought admission, he adds, "And I wanted everyone to know you're mine."

My pulse is beating louder than the noise filling the arena. Did Luke just call me his, or was it a figure of speech? I open my mouth to say something, anything, but am cut off by a chuckling Coach Tavish entering the box.

"All right, Romeo, go cool off in the locker room. Strategy time."

Luke nods, shoots me a wink, and walks expertly away on his skates and down the tunnel. I stare off in wonder with what I can only assume is a goofy grin on my face. It takes Asif's repeated calls on the radio to snap me out of my stupor. Scrambling, I review the next item on my list and get back to work.

I knew this was going to be an amazing night!

20

JAX

IMAGINE your butt is superglued to this seat! I'm so anxious that picturing my mental command does little to control my fidgeting.

Today is the final day of our Communications Seminar, which means Professor Clark will be announcing her summer internship winner. Right now, she's thanking everyone for our ingenuity and yada, yada. I can hardly concentrate. Get to it already!

"The materials and results submitted are the finest I've seen yet," Professor Clark elaborates, making eye contact with each of us as she paces in the front of the room. "I've reviewed your results, and I couldn't be prouder of a group of students than I am of all of you. The score sheets I'm passing out reflects this."

My mouth hurts from the big smile I have stretched across my face, but when I turn to give a thumbs-up sign to Cal Chase, my elation slips. From the second I rushed into the classroom, Cal has been trying to catch my eye. But whatever he wants to say, likely something about April, can wait till later.

The reason why I barely had time to spare this morning has me drawing in my bottom lip to keep from giggling. It felt so nice and cozy sleeping next to Luke's big body that I slept in, which made it harder to sneak out of the Sports House since some of the guys were already up and about for a change.

Fortunately, only Diego spotted me leaving. He laughed and gave me a wink, murmuring how the Ice Man better be in a good mood for once. Considering my sleepovers only make Luke grumpier, I told him not to get his hopes up.

"I'd be feeling lit as fuck right now and thanking my lucky stars!" Diego assured me, reminding me of why I'd originally been charmed by the player. Even if he's full of shit, he sure is good at it.

I'm brought back to the moment I've been waiting for when Professor Clark approaches my row and passes out our grades. Without reviewing the breakdown, my gaze scrolls down to the cumulative score, and I hold my breath to keep from cheering when I see a 98 percent tallied in a red pen at the bottom.

Has anyone scored higher? Cal, thankfully, turns and shows me that he received a ninety-six but mouths the word "sorry." Weird. I shake my head and show him my grade. Nothing to be sorry about, sweetie. Moving on, I peek over the shoulders of the girls in front of me and spot an eighty-three and a ninety-one. I shift my prying gaze to Henry on my left, but he has his paper flipped over and his face hidden behind his hands. I'm going to go out on a limb and cancel him out.

There are only a handful of students left in this small seminar, and since we've been sharing our successes along the way, I haven't seen any evidence to make them a true threat. Yes, I realize I sound more than a tad overconfident, and maybe even arrogant here, but my results and this grade speak for themselves. I even went the extra mile of submitting a letter of praise from Coach Tavish along with my paperwork.

Professor Clark clears her throat to gain attention, and all heads shift back to her. "I'm excited to announce that the highest grade went to Ms. Jacquie Silva for her work promoting the Thatcher Thunderblades, followed by Mr. Cal Chase, whose ideas have already set better pedestrian safety standards on campus. Congratulations, you two!" Clark announces while clapping, which results in a round of applause from the rest of the room.

Wow! Okay, so I guess that means … I earned the internship award!

When I smile over at Cal, his eyes are wide, like he's trying to silently warn me again about something. I quirk an eyebrow in question, but Professor Clark continues, and I pivot, returning my full attention to her. "You're both welcome to come to me if you need recommendations or references in the future."

I smile nervously, not really taking her praise in. A recommendation? Not an internship? I can feel the blood draining from my face and a sickening pit forming in my stomach.

"I just spoke with Cal," Professor Clark continues, "and he's declined participating in the internship contest since he has an iron in the fire already with his previous marketing internship. Well done."

Cal inclines his head coolly, and my stomach churns. It's completely unlike him to be frosty to anyone, never mind a teacher. Something is very off here.

"Which leaves—" Again, people begin to clap, but before I can rise from my seat, Professor Clark's words are like an arrow pinning me back down. "Which leaves me in a difficult position."

Why? It shouldn't be difficult; I have an almost perfect grade! What's the problem?

"While my choice has come down to the highest grade previously, I also have to factor in conduct, ethics, and professionalism, especially when placing a student in a corporate setting, which is why I must look beyond mere grades."

Excuse me? Is she implying that I don't meet these standards? My mind takes this particular moment to produce an image of me in my teapot costume, but angrily, I erase it. That only proves my dedication to a project and the lengths I'd go.

"After weighing the whole package, this summer's internship program goes to Ms. Sophia Palma!"

My mouth falls open, but I'm having problems sucking in air. After a brief pause, the room erupts with applause. In front of me, Sophia, with her ninety-two, is screeching and hugging her friend. A nasty part of me wants to point out that Sophia is hardly acting professionally currently, but I collect myself and manage to clap too.

This time, when I meet Cal's eyes, they are filled with sympathy. His odd behavior earlier now makes sense. He knew Clark wasn't going to choose me, and he was trying to tell me. I look away because his pity and understanding might be my undoing. And although I want to run out of the room the second we are dismissed, the rage simmering inside me keeps me glued to my seat for real. Nope, I'm not going anywhere … not until I speak with my former favorite teacher.

"Yes, Ms. Silva?" Professor Clark asks when I'm the only student remaining. "You did great work this year. You should really be proud of yourself and how much you've helped to build the Thunderblades' reputation not only on campus but throughout the NCAA."

I nod because yes, I did great work, and yes, I am proud, but I'm also freakin' livid. "If my work was so great, why didn't I get the internship?" Yup, my barely there filter has fled altogether.

"I listed my reasons," Clark says, crossing her arms and resting a hip on her desk.

I take a deep breath to calm myself so I don't end up whining, which obviously would be the opposite of demonstrating that I'm mature and professional. "And how exactly did my conduct not measure up?"

"Well, let me ask you this," Professor Clark says, her voice taking on an edge I haven't heard previously. "Do you think it's in good conduct or professional to kiss your client while you are working and in front of all to see?"

I've never been punched in the stomach before, but it sure feels like I was. "But ... but ..." I sputter. "It was just an intermission stunt to engage the audience."

"Yes, a clever one that we approved of in our workshop," Clark says with a stern nod, "but there was no mention of you and your point of contact being among the featured."

"But I didn't know the Kiss Cam was going to target us."

"Weren't you the one to boast about being friends with the head of AV?"

"Yes, Asif and I *are* friends, but I swear I didn't arrange for that! I had no choice but to play along."

"Are you saying you're not carrying on a relationship with the Thunderblades' team captain?"

Am I? He whispered that I was his, but what does that mean? Regardless, the idea of denying how I truly feel is making me ill. Besides, no matter my response, it all seems futile. Defined or not, Luke is more than my "point of contact." There is no refuting that.

I'm almost glad when Professor Clark speaks again before I can come up with a valid answer. "For all intents and purposes, your point of contact was technically your *client*, and you carried out a less than ethical relationship in front of your boss and colleagues, i.e., me and your fellow students."

Ugh, it's not like I kissed Coach Tavish. Luke is my peer, my … Technically, the whole team was my client and I only kissed one out of twenty-five, so that's 4 percent. Great, Jax. You choose now to start being good at calculating percentages?

"Rest assured," Professor Clark resumes over my head trash, "I didn't let this information affect your grade. Your results were stellar despite your lapse in judgment, but unfortunately, I cannot wholeheartedly reward you with an internship in a professional setting at this time."

"I hear what you're saying," I state as calmly as possible, "but I'd never kiss someone while at an actual job and would never have a relationship with a real client. It's just Luke—"

"Stop." Clark holds up a hand for peace. "Consider this a learning opportunity because in the real world, the consequences would be worse, not to mention damaging to your reputation. Now, I must leave for vacation. I hope you have a productive holiday break, Jacquie."

Gee, thanks. I'd much rather *break* apart this room than go home for the winter vacation without the excitement of knowing I'd secured her summer internship. Clark's stupid contest was the dangling carrot I'd been aiming for, my sole purpose this year, and I failed. No, I sabotaged it by getting tied up with a boy. Like mother, like daughter. Following their dreams instead of my own. Dammit!

Luke would never have let this happen if our situations were reversed. He wouldn't have missed his shot just because of whatever it is we are to each other. He'd have had the resolve to stay clear of me and would have focused solely on his objective. Hell's bells, he's been in the right headspace all along. No relationships, no sex, not with his future on the line. Me, on the other hand … I just blew it, and for what? Is this even anything substantial? Are we real?

I don't remember the walk across campus, and I'm surprised when I look up to see Luke standing near my door, holding a pink box of donuts and wearing a big smile that I can't return.

LUKE

As soon as I lay eyes on Jax, my excitement surges to a whole new level, which is already quite high given the news I'm here to deliver. Her being oblivious to my presence only adds to my eagerness to shock her. But she's so lost in thought, she doesn't notice me until she's standing a mere foot away.

"There she is," I say, regretting that I'm holding a box of donuts and unable to scoop her up and twirl her around like I have the insatiable urge to do.

I was hoping for one of her amazing smiles, but instead, Jax looks confused and far away, even though she's staring up at me, or rather past me. I try to think about anything that I've done to make her mad, but my mind draws a blank so I push the negative thought away.

"Come on," I cajole when she still doesn't greet me. "'Donut' worry, these are for you," I joke, extending the pink box filled with her favorites out to her, but she doesn't take them. Am I the only one registering the irony of me pushing donuts and not the other way around?

Before she can respond, my phone rings, and I shift the

box to balance on one hand and grab my cell from my pocket. It's Cal again. "Sorry, it's the second time Cal has called me," I explain, which is odd because, like most guys, we normally text only. With a shake of my head, I select one of the pre-drafted commands that reads: 'Busy, can't talk right now.'

Cal's response is immediate. "Good luck!"

Huh? He couldn't have heard about my announcement —not when I haven't signed on the bottom line yet, not until our family lawyer reviews it.

"You could have answered it," Jax says with a shrug, her face expressionless. Reaching behind me without touching or even brushing my sleeve, she opens the door to her room and enters, not looking back. I can't help but feel like there is something big I'm missing here, and the control freak in me is on high alert.

"I'll talk to him later," I say, following her inside. "Because I want you to be the first person to know."

"Know what?" she questions, finally sounding somewhat interested, but it's hardly her normal enthusiastic curiosity that I've gotten used to.

It's as if Jax knows something that I don't, and she's avoiding telling me what it is. She's also avoiding making eye contact, which again is not like the brazen beauty I know and lov—

"Is there something you want to tell me first?"

Jax's rigid posture crumbles, and my lungs constrict upon witnessing the parade of painful emotions that cross her distraught face. Like I'm passing a puck, I ditch the box of donuts with a flick of my wrist onto her surprisingly tidy desk. Before I can complete the pass, Jax flops down on her made bed and buries her head beneath a pillow.

Forget warning bells. There is a siren going off in my head and I have no clue what to do next, so I hover for a couple of beats. Cautiously, I sit down beside her, unsure what to say. After a moment, she turns on her side, almost in the fetal position, and tosses the pillow across her room where it lands with a soft thud. I'm relieved I wasn't her target, but I'm clueless as to where her anger is really being aimed.

Reaching up, I soothe back the wisps of hair trying to attack her face. Once cleared, she gives me a wobbly smile as tears pool in her eyes. Still, she remains mute. Who knew I'd prefer her endless talking to silence? Desperate for it even? I battle the urge to shake her and get her speaking again.

"What's wrong?" I urge once more.

"You should have answered Cal's calls so he could have told you," Jax says between sniffles, "because now, I can't say it."

WTF? This has to do with Cal? An irrational burn of jealousy courses through me. What could my friend possibly have to tell me in connection to Jax? One possible answer has my hands balling into fists, along with unwanted images popping to mind. I take a deep breath and try to push the idea away, but it won't budge. "You two are seeing each other," I state flatly, sounding a lot like the unfeeling robot I became after my mother died.

"What?" Jax shouts, scrambling up to sit on her knees. "No! Oh my God, no. He's sweet and all, but no. And oh my gosh, April would kill me. She can claim to be a feminist of the highest order, but she'd scratch my eyes out."

It takes around her third no for me to breathe normally again. Obviously, I'm relieved she's not hooking up with my best friend, but I'm even happier to hear her sounding like her usual spirited self, convoluted explanations and all.

"No," she says a final time and then shoves me with

two hands. Thanks to the springy mattress, though, I rock back to her, and when I do, I pull her in for a bear hug. She's now sort of laughing and crying into my chest, and I feel like a dumb idiot because I still have no idea what the hell is going on. I'm about to demand that she clue me in already when she pulls back and looks up at me. Finally! Being able to look into her eyes again feels more rewarding than getting signed by the NHL. I didn't realize until now how badly I needed them, her.

"I got," she begins, her voice hitching, "the highest grade in my Communications Seminar."

"That's wonderful!" I exclaim, unable to mask my confusion. I swear, this girl can sure make a smart guy feel dumb. "But why are you upset? Isn't that great news?"

"Because I didn't get the internship," she blurts out, sagging into me.

"Why not?" Staggered, I let her talk without comment while she rehashes what happened in class earlier, along with a play-by-play of her infuriating discussion with her professor afterward. For the most part, I am following, but my blood is boiling in outrage. All because of the Kiss Cam? This is why I should leave the surprising up to her because, evidently, I'm no good at it.

"This is my fault," I admit, feeling helpless, and my mind rushes to solve this mess. The internship was important to her, and my stomach churns, knowing I'm the one who screwed it up. Nope, it doesn't sit well, especially when she's helped me so much.

"No," Jax says with a long sigh, "it's not. It's mine. And it is what it is."

"I'll go speak with Clark and explain."

I didn't realize I'd started to rise till Jax shoves my shoulders back down, anchoring me next to her. Albeit a puny anchor.

"Don't you dare!" Jax cries. "That will only make things worse. I still have another year left, and despite this, I'm sticking with communications. There's always next time."

But next year, I won't be here. At least not at Thatcher. "There must be something I can do. Or maybe Coach Tavish?"

"It's over." Jax shakes her head, her face resolute. "Besides, what can you say? That we're not romantically involved?"

"Yes!" I agree, nodding my head, but Jax's face pales further. "Your personal life is none of your professor's damn business."

Panic claws at my chest when Jax averts her eyes again and inches away from me. How do I fix this? Despite her words and her acceptance of her professor's unfair verdict, I'm not buying it. I saw the blame in her eyes and can feel Jax's hurt and resentment. Before I can figure out what to say to make things right, though, Jax lies back down where her pillow would have been if not currently living on the floor.

"Sorry, I'm not much company right now," she says with her eyes closed tight. "Maybe you should go."

Ouch! I start to argue, but then I put myself in her shoes. If I had a similar blow, I'd want to be alone too. "Don't be sorry," I tell her, leaning down to press a kiss to her forehead, then rise to stand. "I get it. I'll get out of here so you can ... chill, but we'll figure it out. I promise."

Her eyes flutter open, and within her hazel depths, I can read what she thinks of my promise. Zilch. Knowing actions speak louder than words, I don't push it further. I just need to figure out what those actions are. My resolve might not move her, but it's calming me. With purpose now, I walk toward the door. I'll solve this problem.

"See ya," Jax calls out, dismissing me.

The flippant way she says goodbye feels final, and it has me stopping mid-stride. "I'll see you tomorrow," I correct.

She turns on her side. "You're done with your finals and hockey till January. Aren't you going home?"

"I can drive back anytime," I tell her. "Your flight to California isn't till Sunday, right?"

"Yeah," she says, which I suppose is better than a nod. Great, and now adding to my growing list of fuck ups, I'm feeling guilty for all the times I gave her one-word responses too. That was before though. Before Jax came barreling into my life like a boiling teapot, back when I was still the Ice Man. But she went and thawed that guy, frozen in time, and I've felt lighter ever since. I need to show her how much when she's ready to hear me out.

"Good. We have two more days then," I say fiercely, "and I was hoping to take you out now that we're both free."

She leans up on her elbows, and when she looks at me directly, like she does, I swear my breath catches. "Like a date?" she asks, sounding skeptical.

"Yes, a date," I reiterate, my eyebrow arching at her confusion.

"A real date?" she questions.

I can't help the frustrated laugh that escapes my lips. "Of course. What else would it be?"

Her expressive face informs me that evidently, it could be a lot of things. Ugh, I take it all back. Women are complicated distractions, even Jax, but without her? I don't let myself go there because it's a non-issue, right?

"Okay," Jax says, perking up, and I breathe a sigh of relief. But before I can turn the door handle, she asks, "Was that what you wanted to tell me?"

"Um." Clueless as I may be when it comes to Jax, I

know this isn't the time to share my win. I was hoping we'd both be celebrating tonight, but it looks like we'll have to stick a pin in that for the time being. "No, but it can wait," I reassure her.

She nods but doesn't press, which is also odd, but I take the tiny victory and leave.

After all, I have some calls to make ASAP because if she wants a "real" date, then I'm going to deliver a breakaway goal to top all dates. I never expected to feel this way so soon, but high risk equals high reward, and it's time to pull out all of them for Jax.

For us.

Damn, but it's been a long time since I've wanted something, really wanted something, for myself. And fuck do I want Jax. More than a perfect MCAT score, more than a prime draft pick, just … more. More of her. More of us.

With determined strides I eat up the crosswalk back to my house, blazing a trail quicker than if I was on skates. I'm smiling again too, because if I've learned anything, if it's within my control, I can make it happen.

And I will.

2 2

JAX

CHEER THE F UP, Jax! You've wallowed all last night and most of today. Enough. So, you didn't get the internship. Big deal. It's not the end of the world. No one died. It's just a minor setback. Clark said she'd still provide you with a recommendation, and you have Coach Tavish's letter and stellar results from your Thunderblades' campaign.

You can spend the holidays soliciting alumni on LinkedIn and reaching out to every PR contact in New England if need be. You'll find another opportunity.

Mom's new digs, at least the photos she'd sent, look pretty dope. An ideal place to reset. Besides, it's not like you know anyone in San Diego outside of your mom and the only plans you've made are to head to the beach. You could troll the job boards of your favorite brands while you sunbathe.

But that's for later. Now you have a mystery date with your very own hockey hunk. And if that doesn't fix your vibe, then you need your head examined during the holiday break too.

Merely thinking of Luke has my heartbeat accelerating.

It's kind of a sickening feeling actually, but I can't seem to squelch it no matter how much I order myself to be cool. Maybe it's payback for teasing Emerson and April because now I think I've got it worse than they do. My stomach is so full of nerves that I'm barely eating lately, which alone is a major warning sign, especially for a junk food addict like me.

If this is what it means to "catch feels," then I'm not so sure it's a good thing. Then again, the idea of saying goodbye to Luke tomorrow has me wanting to vomit. I've always prided myself on being the type of woman who didn't need anything serious. Who didn't need a relationship to feel happy. But it only took spending little over a month with Luke for all of that to change.

I guess, no matter what, I'm screwed at this point. Yup, after serial dating, I'm now the one in over my head. I just hope I'm not swimming in the deep end alone. No more pussyfooting around. Tonight, I plan to find out.

I have no qualms about fighting dirty though. For an extra boost of confidence, I'm dressed in a killer, spandex-like, champagne-colored dress that shows off all my curves and brings out the golden-amber hues in my hair. Even if the material cuts off my circulation, it's worth it. All the more satisfying, knowing I got this miracle suit for free from a recent fashion collaboration. It still hurt to cut off the three-hundred-dollar price tag though. No returning or selling this baby, so hopefully, it pays me back with Luke's lusty appreciation.

Pacing in my dorm room, I check the clock on my phone for the third time in the last ten minutes. Luke's text said to be ready by five thirty tonight. Having finished my last exam for the semester this morning, I've been ready for over an hour already.

Eager to get our date started, I head outside to the

parking lot ten minutes early and am yanking the door handle to the passenger side of his SUV before he can do more than turn off the ignition. When I slide into the seat alongside him, I shoot him a smile, but he's scowling.

"I was going to come up and get you," he admonishes. "Or, at the very least, open the car door for you."

As if he did both of those things, I melt inside. "Save the chivalry for Cinderella," I tell him, all bark, no bite. "But thank you just the same."

He huffs out a breath of annoyance and starts the engine back up. Now that I know him better, I recognize his irritation is nothing to be concerned about. Heck, I find it cute even. Grinning, I buckle my seat belt before he can tell me to.

Luke's light-brown hair looks styled tonight and tucked back behind his handsome ears. Yup, I called his ears handsome, and I'm not mad at it. His usual manly scent, meanwhile, is heightened with a musky cologne I haven't smelled before. I inhale the intoxicating notes, and I'm already addicted. Hmm ... seems I'm not the only one playing unfairly.

Automatically, I hum along to a love song on the stereo before I register that it's not his usual, angsty playlist. The dashboard display reveals that he's listening to "Jax's Mix," and I bite back a smile of pure delight. He's playing the songs I like most, and I'm not even sure how he knew which ones to add. The current song is one I used in a not-too-recent video, but that would mean he's viewed my profile. I know that doesn't sound like a big deal, but it means a lot to me. My friends are always rolling their eyes about my social media pursuits, but Luke has never once made fun of them or asked to be involved either. It's kind of the perfect middle ground.

"Where are we going?" I ask eagerly, almost bopping up and down in my seat. But when I see him hit the indicator light and pull into the skating rink, my smile fades and I quickly work to retrieve it. All right, so it's not a fancy dinner. I didn't even want that anyway. But I was hoping for something different. At least not where most of our time together has been spent so far, outside of the team bus and the Sports House, that is.

"I want to show you something," he placates, then parks up front in the reserved spot for Coach Tavish.

I jump when he clamps a warm hand over mine, preventing me from releasing the button on my seat belt. "Wait … please?" he asks, shaking his head, causing the strands of his silky hair to fall forward and escape from behind his ears. I'm too stunned to argue, especially when he brushes an even warmer kiss across my lips. Damn, he tastes better than sugar. It takes the abrupt sound of his front door shutting before I notice he's left me smooching the air. Mesmerized, my gaze follows him as he crosses over to my side, opens the door for me, and reaches over to pop open the seat belt.

"Tricky," I point out, and he chuckles. At the small of my back he places a hand, which I can feel the heat from even through my down jacket, and leads me toward the entrance. With the rink being closed for the break, the rest of the lot is empty, and I'm skeptical that we'll be able to get in. But then Luke pulls out a ring of official keys, selects the dirtiest-looking one, and places it into the padlock and then another into the front door, unlocking it.

When we enter, the familiar chill hits me, and I'm glad he's gripping my elbow since it's pitch black inside, but Luke doesn't hesitate. He places me near the ice entrance and brushes another quick kiss, this time on the top of my head. "Stay right here," he instructs, his voice deep and serious. I nod, but I doubt he can see the movement since it's so dark. A minute later, I hear a switch flip, and a silvery light shimmers across my vision, filling the arena with dancing movement. I glance up to see the disco ball reflecting and circling above, showering us with magical, spinning slivers of light.

Luke returns to my side. "Right this way, madam," he says formally, ushering me onto the ice.

I'm about to object because with the heels I'm wearing, I'll slip and break my neck if I step onto the ice. But when I look down, I see white rose petals scattered across a red carpet train leading out to the middle of the rink. Stunned, I allow him to gently tug me forward. Our arms linked, we walk toward the center where a platform sits.

"Is that the stage from The Cloister?" I ask in disbelief.

"Yup, figured they won't be needing it until next year," he says, gripping me under my arms and lifting me up onto it, then stepping up to join me easily. Unlike the simple, black, wooden box that Steel and April have performed on, the surface is covered with layers of blankets and several pillows. It's beautiful and inviting. And off to the side is a to-go pizza carton from A Piece of My Heart restaurant and another pink box of donuts, which doesn't make any sense. None of this does, but I'm beaming from ear to ear at the pleasant absurdity of it all.

Twirling, I turn to him and ask, "What did you do?"

His smile is boyish. "When I was a kid, I used to tell my parents I wanted to sleep on the ice, but they argued it couldn't be done. When you said you wanted a real date, I tried to think up something special and ..." He waves a hand at the fairy-tale scene he created. "Do you like it?"

"No," I tell him with a sober look that I can barely

hold on to before smiling. "I love it! This is the most romantic thing anyone has ever done for me. It's like *Sixteen Candles*," I gush.

Luke shoots me a confused look. "I have two candles," he says, stepping back down on the ice to light them. "Thanks for reminding me."

The candles add an even more magical glow to this incredible ice picnic. I feel so off balance that for a second, I worry I might faint like I did in psych class, but out of excitement, so I shake my head to clear my excited dizziness.

"No," I say, giggling. "*Sixteen Candles* is an 80s movie."

"Never saw it," Luke says, stepping up close to me. Impulsively, he grabs a fistful of my jacket and pulls me the last inch toward him, then unzips and removes the outer layer for me, carefully laying it on top of the blankets for extra padding. When he turns around again, Luke's head snaps back, as if I'd hit him, and air rushes through his nostrils like an agitated dragon. If his heavy breathing and dilated pupils are any indication, it's safe to say he approves of my dress.

"Oh, you have to," I tell him, but my voice quivers.

"Have to what?" he murmurs absently, his gaze roving up and down my body.

"See the movie," I say with a laugh.

He shrugs. "If you'll watch it with me."

"Netflix and chill?" I tease with suggestion, and Luke's eyes darken when they meet mine. That sexy beast look he gets when he's out on the ice crosses his features, and I can feel myself getting wet in response. Hot damn, that look can melt the ice around us or, at the very least, my panties.

I squeak in surprise when Luke springs forward and collects me in his arms. His hot kiss stifles the laughter rising in my throat. Instead, my giggle bubbles out like a needy groan. I hold on to him to keep my balance when my knees try to give way, but one of Luke's strong hands runs down my spine to anchor me.

Our kiss turns feverish—fast. My entire body feels on fire with need for him. Panting, Luke breaks off from my mouth and I sink into his chest, not wanting the loss of contact.

"Fuck, Jax! I can't concentrate when you're wearing that, and I have shit to say."

Hugging me, he lowers us down and sits cross-legged on a pillow. My dress doesn't allow me to do the same, so I extend my bare legs out in front of me, crossing them at the ankles. With a muffled curse, Luke frames my shoulders with a blanket, tucks it around me, and drapes another over my legs, covering me up from his view. He nods as if satisfied with his work now that I look like a mummy, then shoves a hand roughly through his hair.

"Okay, where do I begin? You got me so mixed up that I forgot how I'd rehearsed it."

"Sorry," I say, but my smile belittles my apology. He's practiced what he's about to say? How adorable. I do the same in the mirror all the time but didn't expect him to.

"No, you're not," he says with a frustrated laugh before placing yet another quick kiss on my forehead this time. I'm eating up how affectionate he is being. It's almost as if he can't help himself. I know I'm unable to resist him, but this is the first time I'm beginning to think he can't either.

"Your internship!" he blurts out, recalling his first talking point, and my smile fades at the dark cloud infiltrating this dream. "I'm sorry about that. I had no idea the Kiss Cam stunt would get you in trouble. I was trying to surprise you like you constantly do to me. I told you, though, we'd figure it out, which brings me back to the big news I wanted to share with you yesterday."

Luke pauses to collect his thoughts, and I nod encouragingly. "I feel terrible I didn't let you tell me—"

"Shh," he murmurs, cutting me off by pressing the pads of his fingers into my lips. His gaze falls to my mouth, and he quickly drops his hand away. "Believe it or not, I like hearing you talk because I never know what you're about to say next. But let me get all this out, will you?"

Dutifully, I nod, although what I really want to do is capture his fingers between my teeth and kiss him all over. So, I gently bite the inside of my cheek instead and bide my time.

"I received an offer to join the Boston Bluebacks and I've verbally accepted, only some paperwork left to do."

"What? Oh my gosh, you did it!" Unable to stay still, I launch myself into his arms, which wrap fiercely around me. I pepper him with congratulatory kisses up and down his face, which he then takes several layers deeper.

My eyes are blurry when I let go of his bottom lip, and my mind races to process his incredible news. Wow! He's going to the NHL. "But does this mean you're not going to finish your last semester at Thatcher after all?"

Yes, evidently, I can be elated for him and miserable for me at the same time. I of course knew he'd be graduating soon, but I still wanted these next couple of months together, and the thought of not seeing him anymore has my gut plummeting.

"No, it's a special agreement that will allow me to graduate first, then head to training camp in June, barring any injuries on my part, which would nullify the terms. I won't be able to collect a salary or a sign-on bonus until that time, either, but I'm not concerned about that. Paul had said no team would go for it, yet the Bluebacks were my first pick and they did. All without an agent taking a portion either."

"That's absolutely perfect," I gush. He's perfect. Unable to contain the thought, I tell him so, but he just shakes his head almost shyly. Told you. Me, on the other hand … ugh, I have work to do, starting with snapping out of my selfish funk. "And you've been holding this news in because I didn't win a stupid internship?" I point out with a groan.

Luke lifts my falling chin, so I meet his eyes. "Your internship wasn't stupid," he corrects, "which brings me to the next thing on my list to share with you."

While he pauses to gather his thoughts, my stomach growls. "I hope your list includes sharing pizza too?"

Chuckling, Luke reaches for the box, flips it open, hands me a cheese slice, and grabs one with the works for himself. We both fold the crust and tap our slices together in a sort of pizza cheers before taking a bite. Yup, perfect just got perfecter. Mmm.

No plates, so we use the carton as one big communal one. When we're done, he tosses the box onto the ice, where it slides a few extra feet, then we split a sparkling water.

"All right, now that's done," Luke says, continuing his speech. "I spoke with the Bluebacks' communications head and told her about what you did for the Thunderblades. She said she'd love to have a college intern like you this summer on her team and to give her a call right after New Year's. Oh, and I know you were counting on housing, too, but since they'll be providing me with an apartment, you can always room with me. You'll get to travel with us, too, when your schedule allows."

I pause, processing this. Room and an internship—everything I wanted—and I'd be near Luke too. It's better than any scenario I could have imagined or found myself. The Bluebacks are a major brand, too, and could very well be a better fit for me than Clark's mysterious company this summer. Still, something is nagging at me, telling me this doesn't feel right.

"But I didn't earn it," I say, shaking my head.

Luke's grip on my waist tightens a smidge. "Of course you did. They don't give every player's girlfriend a job, you know. I sent over your report, your videos, and told them how you helped grow our social following and notoriety for Frost Fest. Tavish also forwarded the letter he gave to Clark. So, hell yes, YOU earned this, Jax, just like you deserved to win Clark's internship in the first place."

My mouth opens and closes. This is a lot to take in. And girlfriend? This shouldn't be the part to focus on, but I do.

"You hear me?" Luke asks, shaking my shoulders gently for emphasis when I still haven't responded. "This is all you. We just happen to be dating, that's all."

"Girlfriend? Dating?" Crap, I went and echoed that aloud. My bad, but this is uncharted territory for me.

Luke looks incredulous. "Well, yeah, aren't you? I mean, aren't we?"

"Do you want me to be?" I hedge.

Luke groans loudly. "God, woman, you're frustrating," he says, pinching the bridge of his nose, "but I wouldn't take it any other way. Yes, I want you to be my girlfriend. Didn't I kiss you in front of the whole school and tell you that you were mine? Weren't you listening?"

I nod. "Yeah, I heard you, but like, for real?"

"What is it with you and that word? A real date. Real girlfriend. It's always been real between us, Jax. Haven't you felt it? I've never had to fake anything or be anyone but myself with you. Even when I tried to freeze you out or literally close the door on you, you wouldn't let me."

Tears are gathering in my eyes, but I laugh because I stubbornly did do that. Taking my hands in his, Luke continues. "In the six weeks I've known you, you've made me feel lighter and happier than I've felt in years. You're everything I have been missing."

"I'm glad I was able to do that for you," I tell him, squeezing his hands in return. "But now, you're going to be a pro athlete, traveling and living it up, and I'll still be a lame college student stuck here for another year. You don't need me or a relationship holding you back."

Luke scoffs. "First of all, you couldn't be lame if you tried. Secondly, holding me back? I was doing that all by myself. If it weren't for you, I'd still be struggling with my promise to my mother and wondering if hockey should be my future or just a hobby. Thirdly, I'm not sure what me going pro has to do with anything. I'm sure as hell not interested in anyone else, if that's what you're thinking."

"Maybe not now, but you're going to have women throwing themselves at you—"

Tugging on my hands, he pulls me back onto his lap and into a tight hug. "You're picturing roadblocks before they even happen. Won't happen, in fact!"

"I'm just being realistic," I argue into his chest, rubbing my cheek into his soft sweater to wipe away my falling tears that I couldn't keep in any longer. When he brushes a kiss across the top of my head, it takes all my willpower to keep from bawling.

"No, this is you trying to leave me before I leave you. Well, good luck with that because I won't let you."

"What?" Great, now I'm laughing and crying like some unhinged lunatic. "That's not how it works."

"Too bad. I go after what I want, and if I haven't

made it clear enough, I want *you*." Bending his head, Luke's lips find mine in a tender kiss. His hands cup my face as he deepens it and my toes curl in my shoes, overwhelmed with the emotion of it all. "This wasn't on my list to share tonight," Luke says, dragging his lips in a sensual line to my ear, "but I suppose I have nothing to lose since I've already lost my heart to you. I love you, Jacquie Silva!"

I gasp, my lungs constricting in a blissful sort of pain I've never experienced before. Pulling back, I search his face and see only truth. I didn't realize how good it would be to hear those words, to have the warmth of them flow over me, but I suspect finally saying them in return will be even better.

"Don't worry," Luke soothes. "There's no pressure to say it back. I know you want to wait until—"

"Shh," I hush, stilling him by putting my fingers on his lips this time. Why shouldn't I say it and take the plunge too? I'm not my mother. I know my own heart and it's hammering for Luke, to where I can barely contain it in my chest. "Can I talk now?" He nods his head, my fingers moving with the action. "Thanks for calling me out on my bullshit because yes, I guess that's what I was trying to do. What I've always done. I've been telling myself I don't love you, that it's just a crush, but this feeling is not going away. And I've never felt like this before, so wishy-washy or this insecure, this horrible!"

"Gee, thanks," Luke mumbles, but he's smiling wide, and I know he understands. I move my hands to grip his shoulders, and our eyes meet and hold.

Unable to break his gaze, I tell myself to let go and for once I listen.

"I can't stop thinking about you, and I both hate and crave it." I continue gazing into his clear, blue eyes that I once stupidly thought were cold. "And deep down, I know it's because I love you too."

The words rush out before I even realize it, but I'm glad I said it. He touches his lips to my forehead, just between my eyebrows. The moment is so sweet that if I hadn't just had the courage to say I love you, it surely would have escaped now. Overwhelmed, my lips meet his, and I try to pour every bit of love I'm feeling into our kiss.

"Don't forget who said it first," Luke says with a smirk when he pulls back an inch. "And," he prods, his lips twitching with amusement, "you forgot to add, 'Luke, I'm not interested in seeing anyone else either,'" he says, mimicking my voice.

Rolling my eyes, I repeat, "And Luke, I'm not interested in anyone else but you."

"Glad we're finally on the same page," Luke says, puffing out his chest. "Now come here."

"I am here," I taunt, wiggling my ass, which is seated atop his lap.

"Careful," he warns with bedroom eyes, his lids hooded. "You're playing with fire."

"Oh really?" I ask, grinding farther into his hard groin. "Fire? I thought they call you the Ice Man."

Luke releases a throaty laugh. "Not anymore. That guy is gone. You went and poured hot tea over him. Also, I have my contract with the NHL now and no more games until next year, which means …"

Luke flips me onto my back, reversing our positions before I can do no more than gasp. Pressing me into the bed of blankets, his hot mouth and fevered hands are everywhere at once. But it's not enough. I need to feel him against me, inside me, skin to skin. Arching, I dig my hands into his firm hips, pressing him closer.

Luke kisses his way down my neck to the pulse in my

throat. Biting gently, he pins me there with his teeth and I shiver with pleasure. "Say it again," he demands. His silky, deep voice slides its way down my spine, bringing my entire body to attention.

I nod, and he releases my tender skin.

"I love you," I tell him, and it's so fucking freeing. As if my heart has sprung wings, I can almost see it flying away along with those three words. "I love you. I love you."

23

LUKE

Jax has gone and surprised me once again. Relief, joy, and pleasure rush through me as she continues to chant that she loves me. Not the hockey star. Me.

When her luscious, ripe body pumps under me, I'm about ready to jump out of my own skin. The taste and feel of her is consuming me, and knowing I don't have to hold back has my hands fumbling, unsure where to explore next.

"You mentioned wanting to sleep out on the ice. Is sleep all that you have in mind?" Jax whispers teasingly into my ear, causing shivers to skate down my spine. Oh, she's going to be a handful and I can't be happier about it.

A deep chuckle reverberates from my chest. Bending lower, I trail my tongue down the slope leading to her cleavage, nipping and kissing every inch of flesh along the way. I can feel goose bumps breaking out on her skin in response.

"I have a lot of things in mind when it comes to you," I admit. "But no, sleep is not one of them."

"Care to share?" she asks, daring me to enumerate them.

Before I can, a lightning bolt of lust strikes my soul when her tongue darts out and traces the inner shell of my ear. Yet, a pesky thought occurs and pushes through my raging hormones. Propping myself up on my elbows, I look down at her dazed face. "Jax, just because I can, and all, I'm not assuming or want you to think I expect anything tonight."

Hope, wish, want, but no expectations.

Her expression clears, and she shoots me an agitated glare. "Oh, but I have a lot of expectations, and I don't know if you've noticed this about me, but I'm not a patient person."

"I've noticed," I confirm, tugging down the straps of her dress, freeing her breasts for my mouth to capture and tongue to circle. I could spend hours here, but she won't let me. Her busy hands move between us to tug up my sweater, her nails scraping wickedly up my back. I help by pulling it up and over my head, adding it to the pile of cushions around us.

Her gaze darts down to my waist, where my full-blown erection strains against the zipper of my pants. Although she's seen it before, she's yet to truly explore him, and the thought has my pulse accelerating and my cock throbbing painfully.

"It's been a while for me," I tell her, my voice thick. "You'll have to excuse me for being in a hurry."

My stomach muscles jump when her cool hand works at the button of my pants, pulling me closer as we fight to keep our mouths together while she hurries to unzip me. "That is so not a problem. I want you—now, Luke!"

I exhale, long and relieved and turned on. I don't have to be told twice. My pants and boxers are off in a flash, discarded somewhere over my shoulder. I yank the remainder of her dress down to her waist, and she helps by slithering the rest of the way out of it. A half growl, half moan rips through my chest when flesh meets flesh, and I realize she has nothing on underneath. I'd already discovered the lack of a bra, but ... "You've been calmly talking to me and wiggling around on my lap with no panties on?"

Her naughty and sexy-as-fuck smile confirms she's going to be the death of me. Letting my hand dance down her long legs to her ankles, I reach for the scrap of fabric that was her dress. "You won't be needing this for some time," I tell her, and toss it out onto the ice.

Scrambling, I stuff a hand underneath one of the pillows and pull out a travel box of condoms.

Jax's mouth forms an O when she spots what I'm holding. "You came prepared."

I give a guilty shrug. "I came hoping, but speaking of cumming ..." Desperate, I place the heel of my palm firmly between her legs, and instinctually, she grinds into me, her head falling back, exposing the line of her throat to my lips and teeth again. From our past episodes of fooling around, I know just how hard and fast she likes it, but she bats my hand away and I look down at her in surprise.

"My turn," she demands, her hand wrapping around my protruding cock.

The air escapes from my lungs in a rush as she delicately traces my shaft and plays with the pre-cum at the tip, spreading the liquid in circles over the head. Stealing the box from my other hand, she removes one and rips it open with her teeth.

Damn, everything she does turns me on further. Impatient now, too, I take over the task and sheath myself with the lubricated condom. The sudden grip sets my teeth on edge, but it's not quite the fit I'm looking for. Reading my mind, or perhaps we're of shared thought, Jax brings me to her warm entrance, then falls back, raising her hips up, urging me forward.

I slide slowly into her, and when I close my eyes from the sweet torture, lights dance behind my eyelids. The feel of her, along with her whimpers, are driving me crazy, to the point where everything I know and need is Jax.

My hips piston in and out, slowly savoring each inch, but when the heels of her feet dig into my ass, pressing me deeper, I ride with her in a fast, sweaty race to fulfillment, my heart thundering. Jax grinds herself against the base of my cock in urgent demand, then stills. Expelling her breath in a rush, Jax slumps her shoulders, and I watch as shocked pleasure rushes over her beautiful face as she pours her release over me. In one last thrust, I drive myself home, pinning her into the cushions and joining her in euphoria.

Quivering, I drop my head in the crook of her neck but am careful not to crush her. Tucking her against me, still joined intimately, I draw us to our sides.

"Are you okay?" I ask, worried I might have been rough for our first time, especially considering this is just a makeshift bed. Although, I was so lost with passion, I'd have taken her up against the glass if need be.

Staring up at the twirling disco ball above, she manages a weak smile. "I'll let you know once I can think again."

Chuckling, I'm distracted by her naked body and skim my hands along her curves, dips, and valleys while she recovers her thoughts. Hopefully, I'm making it harder for her to do so, like she is for me. Literally.

After a few minutes, Jax eases up on her elbows and pins me with an alarmed look. "I should probably have asked this before, but we're alone in here, right?"

"I sure as hell hope so," I say with a bark of laughter. "Everyone has left for the break, but I had locked the door behind us too."

She nods and falls back with relief.

"So," I say, trailing a finger around her pert nipples and then down her belly to the v between her legs. "I believe I promised you a hat trick."

She cocks her head and looks at me warily. "Yes, I believe you did."

"Well, I wouldn't want to start our relationship off by not delivering on my promises," I say as seriously as I can manage, which isn't easy considering where my hand has diverged to.

"No, that would not be good," she says, sounding a bit haughty, then heaves a fake sigh. "I'm just not sure you're up for it, big guy."

Oh ho, so that's how she wants to play it. She dares to pout, too, and I bite down on my own lip to steal myself from leaping forward to punishingly kiss that pout away. Instead, I do a tsk-tsk sound and sink a finger inside her. "Baby, I'm a pro athlete. I recover quickly and am always ready for a rematch. I'm only worried about little you."

As expected, that gets her back up. With an agility that could rival a winger's, Jax has me flat on my back and is sinking down on my newly sheathed cock before I can discard the wrapper.

"We'll see," she boasts with a satisfied smile.

I saw ... and we both won!

EPILOGUE

JAX

You can go ahead and call me Captain Jax because I got my ships in order. Friendships, relationship, and internship. Toot toot!

Hmm, that sounded more like a car horn than a ship's blast. But despite spending the holidays in San Diego and visiting the naval base where my mom's boyfriend works, I can't recall hearing any ship horns to reference.

Turns out though, Greg, that's his name, isn't so bad after all. In fact, he seems genuinely crazy about my mom in return, so that's just another ship I don't have to worry about steering anymore. It only took 21 years, but it appears my mom is in "ship shape" for a change. Alright, I'll stop with the ship metaphors, but mainly because I can't think of any others, and I need to direct Tanner Bouché where to put down my stuff. I point toward the empty closet after noticing the box he's holding, or rather flexing comically is labeled shoes.

Although Luke isn't a Thunderblade anymore or even a student here, he still arranged for his former hockey team to be at my disposal today for my move in. Luke felt guilty that he couldn't help me get settled into my new senior dorm room, but his pre-season games have started and being the NHL rookie to watch, he's under a lot of pressure to perform.

I almost sigh aloud, thinking of him. As if on some sappy command, key memories of our summer together flash through my mind—walking around Boston Common seeking out the best food trucks to try; his hysterical commentary during my fashion videos; spending lazy Sundays in bed till noon. I remind myself that I still have stuff at his place and can drive to see him easy enough, but it's not the same. Yeesh, I know, I've turned into *that* girl. Cut me some slack though, it's the first time in months that I won't be seeing Luke or sharing an apartment with him, and it feels just plain weird. It's like I'm … untethered, and no that wasn't supposed to be a ship reference, but I suppose it fits.

Luke isn't taking the separation any better, but he can at least channel his frustration and bad temper out on the ice. I suppose we'll both be busy though and it's not like we won't be talking every day.

I glance down at my phone. Even though Luke is en route to his game, he's been texting me and asking if I arrived alright. I give a thumbs-up sign to his latest question:

> Luke: Are the guys there to unload your stuff?

His message is followed by a pic of the empty seat next to his on the luxury team bus. It's where I'd normally sit chattering away or trading barbs with the other guys. I swear the Bluebacks are an amazing group and their camaraderie and friendship sort of feels like being part of a big family. Then again, it's also like I gained a dozen older brothers, but for an only child like me, I love it! Still, if one more big brute tries to warn me to buckle my seat belt or to not step out on the ice without skates, I might have to unleash a little sister tantrum. Being the new guy, Luke has had it worse though. Can't lie, it's been funny as hell seeing him at the bottom of the totem pole for a change and getting ribbed by his new teammates.

Although my summer internship with the Boston Bluebacks wrapped up last week, I'm still so thankful as it truly was a dream position. I also loved growing the brand online during the offseason. The best part, of course, was being with Luke and seeing him train and joining on team dinners and outings. Not just as his girlfriend either, but as an extended member of the team.

It sucked saying goodbye to everyone and driving back up to Thatcher today, but after looking at their upcoming schedule, I should be able to attend several of their weekend home games this fall. Also, the Bluebacks will be going up against Chicago over Thanksgiving week, and Kathy is already researching house rentals for the four of us again.

Fingers crossed, I might be a full-time member of the Bluebacks soon. On my last day, I was rendered speechless when instead of simply gaining experience from the temporary internship, it ended with a job offer. Once I graduate and finish my senior year that is. I haven't committed yet, but knowing that I have something lined up post-college has taken an enormous weight off my shoulders.

Meanwhile, Blake Halsey is removing from *his* shoulders my contraband microwave and shakes his head in censure. Yes, I know microwaves aren't allowed, but I've got away with hiding it in my closet these last three years, saving me many trips to the basement to heat-up my Cup O Noodles.

I slap Blake on the back. "Don't worry about it." He only huffs and walks out to collect more of my stuff from downstairs.

"Don't mind him. *I* love a rebel," Tanner says with a wink, and I laugh. Evidently, that's all the encouragement he needed because he shuffles closer. "So, does that mean you subscribe to the out of sight, out of mind theory?"

I shake my head. Tanner is truly incorrigible, but also harmless. Brave too, considering he's the only teammate of Luke's to flirt with me, even after we were official. "When it comes to microwaves and the edibles that I have stored inside my cosmetic bag, yes, but not sneaking behind my guy's back."

"Then let's take this," he says waving a hand between the two of us "out in the open."

My look must say it all, because Tanner lifts his hands in surrender. "Hey, you can't blame a guy for trying."

Cayden, who'd been watching our exchange with unconcealed disgust, deposits my bedding on the empty mattress and slaps Tanner upside the head.

"Ouch!" Tanner whines, nursing the back of his neck, just as my cell phone chirps, indicating another text message.

> Luke: Make sure Tanner doesn't stick around after. No feeding strays

I burst out laughing. What timing. Is my new room bugged? That hockey sense of his. It's damn creepy sometimes.

Blake enters again, his arms laden with my dresses still on hangers, dangling from his big limbs. I gather them from him and put them inside my closet, effectively hiding the illegal microwave.

"I think that's all of it," Blake mumbles from behind me and hands over my car keys.

"Thank you so much guys!"

"If you need anything this year, just holler," Cayden says, and they all nod in agreement.

"I will," I assure them, dolling out hugs as they leave, but once they do, the silence of my room hits me. No Luke, and no roommate this year, either. The latter is a relief, especially if Luke is able to visit. And at least April is in the same building. Emerson though is shacking up with Steel off-campus. Lucky bitch, lol.

> Luke: Oh, and when Cal wraps up with April, he's going to reinstall your door lock.

> Why??

> They break. Don't argue, just be sure and send me a key!

> 

> Ha! A real one.

> What's with you and that word—real? Real date... ;)

> I miss you already. For real.

> Me too. I love you—for real. Xoxo

I love you so freakin much Jax. Now, don't be late for your first editorial meeting.

Yes, sir.

Good luck!

Thank you, you too!

I shoot him over what I hope is a sexy selfie. The string of fire emojis he replies with confirms it. Phew!

Luke is right about me not being late, though. I only have a half hour before I need to head over to the arts building. At the end of last year, I snagged the Arts & Culture editor position at the school paper, the *Thatcher Tribune*. I'm hoping it will round out my communications portfolio and keep me busy outside of class too. Besides, our new editor-in-chief, K.J., is a recent transfer from Michigan and she really wants to shake things up by adding more content. She's even assigned me a monthly fashion advice column, which I'm also excited about.

So, I'm going to take a page out of my Ice Man's book and focus this year. Focus on my classes. Focus on being happy.

Chirp!

Ohh another text!

At first, I'm confused when I see a string of numbers until I click on them and realize it's a confirmation number for a flight booked in my name to Chicago in November.

Smiling, I grab my purse and head, no practically skip, to the arts building.

* * *

Want more of Luke?

Join my newsletter and grab your FREE bonus deleted prologue from Luke's POV before he met Jax and more exclusive content
➡ http://bit.ly/hotandcoldbonus

DRIVES ME CRAZY

A COLLEGE SOCCER OPPOSITES
ATTRACT ROMANCE

CHAPTER ONE

Diego Delarosa

"This is total BS!"

I curse aloud, not caring if I'm overheard, even welcoming the chance to vent some. With no soccer ball in sight, I sidekick a pebble in my path as I jog across Thatcher College's idyllic upper campus.

I can't believe I'm missing the film review of yesterday's game because of this stupid meeting. I was really looking forward to seeing the replay of the sweet bicycle kick I'd managed in the third quarter to score. A perfect shot to add to my highlight reel for the MLS scouts.

An alert dings on my smartwatch, indicating that the team's recap is about to start, which also means I'm going to be late for my appearance at teen court, a.k.a. the student-led review board hearing.

Picking up the pace, I weave and cut through a yoga class that's being conducted outside on the green. It's a crisp fall day in New England, but the sun is out, making it feel warmer than norm for this time of year. Just another reason to be pissed that I won't be out on the field this afternoon. Maybe if I'm lucky I can get this over with quickly, and I'll still make the 5-on-5 scrimmage.

"Watch it!" a girl cries out as I jump over her purple mat, but then her initial, biting voice turns all sweet. "Oh, Diego, it's you."

I don't recognize her, but I slow down for a brief second to admire the view of her doing the downward-facing dog pose. As was her aim, I can spot a Y-shaped outline of a whale tail. Naughty, but I'm here for it, and just like that, my mood lifts. "So sorry," I respond, throwing her 'the look' I perfected since I was ten. It's gotten me out of several jams ... and into more than a couple of relationships. "I wish I could give you a private workout, but I'm late."

She and several of the yogis around her laugh in response.

"Next time!" Yoga chick promises.

Reluctantly, I turn my gaze away and toward the white chapel at the other end of the quad. A foreboding, dark cloud looms behind the steeple now, and I'm hoping it's not a bad sign for what's to come.

Built in 1851, the chapel is the oldest building on campus. Disgusted, I shake my head. How sanctimonious of them to hold their summons in such a holy spot. Intimidation much?

During the first week of school, the signing of our honor code took place inside. And while they still hold non-denominational services, the chapel is mainly used for glee club concerts and alumni gatherings. I pause, realizing I haven't crossed its doorway since my freshman year, three years ago. I shrug. What can I say ... time flies when you're having fun? And that's the thing about time—you either use it or lose it. That's my motto right there!

Disregarding the ramp outside the building, I climb the worn, granite steps two at a time. Never miss an opportunity to get the heart racing. Another policy that I live by.

Parting the heavy, wooden doors, I'm greeted with the sight of an unmanned pipe organ. Dunt dunt dun, I hum under my breath. But I'm already late. No point pissing my executioners off further by singing the melody out loud. Yup, the stiff-looking group seated alongside the podium confirms that my amusement would not be well received.

All eyes are focused on me. Uneasy, I manage to give what I hope is a contrite smile, yet I have the urge to genuflect as I walk down the aisle to where an empty chair is placed, facing the elevated group of four students.

Two faculty members are sitting in the first pew, too. One of which is Mr. Lowe, Thatcher's Dean of Academics, who's been riding the athletic department's ass since I've been here. Just great. Coach Fusco is going to have a field day when he hears about this. This probably doesn't count toward keeping a low profile as Coach instructed when I arrived back on campus this year … his wariness stemming from our school paper recently listing the names of athletes on full-ride sports scholarships at Thatcher College, yours truly included.

The biased editorial argued that academic scholarships, which reward intellectual achievement, should be the priority of our great institution. Blah, blah, blah. As a result, I've been hearing crap from teachers and the anti-sports crowd ever since. Not to mention suddenly, it's like uncool to date a jock. Not that jersey chasers are the reason why I play, but I must admit, it's been a decent perk.

Taking a seat, I nod at the group staring silently back at me. Leading the student review board is senior—and likely this year's upcoming valedictorian—Jin Wei. He's wearing a freakin suit and tie like we're at a funeral.

Shit, are we? My stomach flips. Maybe this will be the death of my college soccer career. With Mr. Lowe being here, I'm not so confident this will be the slap on the wrist I was expecting.

Cringing, I take in the dirty practice jersey that I have on and can hear my dad's voice inside my head, *"You dress for the job you want, mío, not the one you have."* Well, all I ever wanted to be is a soccer player, so done! If college wasn't a means to an end for me, I'd have gladly skipped it and let my little sister be the first in the Delarosa family to matriculate instead. Yet, now that it might be a reality, I'm not so sure I'm cool with it, especially now that I'm just one semester away from graduating. My last season to show up and show off.

The alternative has my chest tightening, and I can feel a case of heartburn coming on. Like I need that? And for fuck's sake, why the hell isn't anyone talking? I know we're in a church, but still. It's so quiet, I can hear the sudden fall of raindrops pelting the roof above and am picturing how the yoga class must be scrambling right about now.

Like me internally, I commiserate taking in my so-called peers once again. On Jin's left is Emerson Powers, a shy girl and another smarty-pants senior. She gives me a kind smile, at least. I don't know her well, but she's cool. I mean, she must be. Her boyfriend is Steel Nash, the son of the rockstar Diesel. Talk about an odd pair.

Next to her, is trust fund bro Trey douchebag the third. How the hell that suck-up is on the review committee is beyond me. He's a walking misdemeanor. No doubt his parents have connections, though, or he bluffed his way in, as usual.

And … fuck me! Rounding out the high-and-mighty foursome is the flawless and always effortlessly put together Valerie Perfect.

Fine, it's Valerie *Perkins*, but it might as well be perfect. All the P's—petite, preppy, president of Theta Kappa Gamma. It doesn't help that she thinks she's special or something because her mom is State Congresswoman Perkins and her dad is a big-deal judge, but at least it explains the silver spoon up her butt. Whatever the reasons, she's not only smart and confident, she's unattainable and impossible to ignore. I know this because I've tried.

From the first moment I saw her, I lost my cool and acted like a cartoon character with my jaw dropping to the floor and my heart practically popping out of my chest. Valerie, on the other hand, has had no problem freezing me out, long before this review summons or the *Thatcher Tribune*'s article was published. Back when I was still a rookie and she was just a pledging freshman finding her way. But now she's the new president of the most popular sorority on campus. As such, I have no doubt she's the main perpetrator of why her house has cut back on Thunder victory parties, except for the hockey team. Why hockey is having a moment, I have no idea. Soccer is played in nearly every country, while hockey is only in around seventy countries, but whatever.

Jin purposefully clears his throat, commanding attention, then robotically reads from a piece of paper listing my four-digit case number like I'm some sort of felon.

"This hearing of the Honor Code Review Board is now officially in session," he states, but when he unexpectedly smacks down a wooden gavel, I almost jump in my chair. What the? Is this an actual court? Should I have an attorney? Am I allowed a phone call? I literally bite my tongue to keep from laughing at the absurdity of it all as, one by one, each member confirms that they are either "here" or "present."

Like seriously, what the fuck?

"We are gathered to examine a potential violation of our institution's academic integrity policy. The accused, Diego Delarosa, is present, along with members of the review board and advisers, to determine the appropriate course of action regarding the alleged breach of conduct."

"Mr. Delarosa, you are brought before this board today due to concerns regarding your enrollment in Ethics 302. It has come to our attention that while you received a passing grade in the course, you did so without ever attending a single session. The honor code explicitly states that students must engage actively and honestly in their coursework."

Jin looks at me predictably, his expression already exasperated. Well, good. I am, too. And while I'm not sure if it's my turn to talk or not, I can't stay quiet a moment longer. "I don't get it. I *honestly* passed, so why does it matter whether or not I wasted valuable time sitting in a classroom?"

"Failing to attend a course while still receiving credit is considered a misrepresentation of academic participation and is in direct violation of our academic honor policy," Jin explains like he's memorized the entire code. The loser probably has.

"I *did* the work, I didn't cheat," I maintain. "My assignments were completed on time, and I submitted what was asked. Isn't that the point?"

"The honor code isn't just about not cheating,"

Emerson chimes in, her voice gentle. "It's about being honest and present in all aspects of your academic journey. By skipping class but still receiving credit, you misrepresented your level of participation."

Before I can contradict this, Valerie speaks up, too, neatly tucking her long, blonde hair back behind her ears. "An ethics class, of all classes," she says with an inelegant snort, "holds the principle of integrity at its core. The concern here is not just attendance, but the integrity of the coursework itself. If we let one person skip out on the very thing the course represents, it sets a dangerous precedent for everyone."

"Oh, yeah, super dangerous," I mock, rolling my eyes. Aight, rein it in, dude. Sarcasm is not going to score you any points here, but Miss Perfect tends to bring out the worst in me. Always has. "I got an 80." Without even trying, I almost add, but I'm not that dense to disclose this fact.

"It's not just about passing, Diego," Valerie placates, her tone calming, and it helps cool my nerves some. At the same time, I'm also suspicious. I didn't count on her being one of my allies today. "It's about participating in the process. Your attendance and engagement are part of what makes this an ethical academic environment for all. By skipping class entirely, you're not being an active member of this community, and that's what's being considered unethical. You weren't just absent from a lecture—you missed the opportunity to engage in dialogue, to learn, and to grow."

That's it! Standing, my chair scoots back, metal screeching on stone. "I don't participate in this community?" I ask, stabbing a thumb at my chest in disbelief. "I'm the starting striker for the Thatcher Thunder, two-time NCAA Division II Men's Soccer

Championship Winners responsible for keeping our college in the Top 10 national rankings. I travel across the country, proudly wearing Thatcher crimson and representing *OUR* school. All of which, I might add, is a huge factor in driving international admissions and maintaining alumni interest."

Yup, sit on that and spin! I heave in a gulp of air, thankful I remembered the last bit of fuel from Coach Fusco's motivational speeches over the years. I never cared much about those aspects of playing, just the wins and the game itself, but I assume and hope the administration will. After all, who wants to go to a school no one's ever heard of? Sports is what keeps Thatcher in the news and gives it street cred, if you will.

END OF EXCERPT
Read Now on KU

Mine to Five (Holiday Office Romance)

Jesse's Girl (Small-Town Romance)

Don't Start Now (Vacation Romance)

It Might Be You (Sweet Short Story)

Blinded Me With Science (Opposites Attract College Romance)

One More Kiss (Enemies-to-lovers College Novella)

Drives Me Crazy (College Soccer Romance)

ABOUT THE AUTHOR

Blogger and former PR executive, Tara holds a master's degree in Journalism and Communications from New York University and a B.A. in English from Wheaton College in Massachusetts. 

An avid romance reader, she has been daydreaming about being a romance author since high school. Dozens of bad dates and adventures later, she still finds it impossible that she met her husband on a NYC subway. Now they live in sunny Southwest Florida with identical twin boys and four distractions (I mean cats) underfoot. When the kids are asleep and the cats are not lying on her keyboard, she's finally writing the happily ever after tales she's been dreaming about.

www.TaraSeptember.com
@TaraSeptemberAuthor